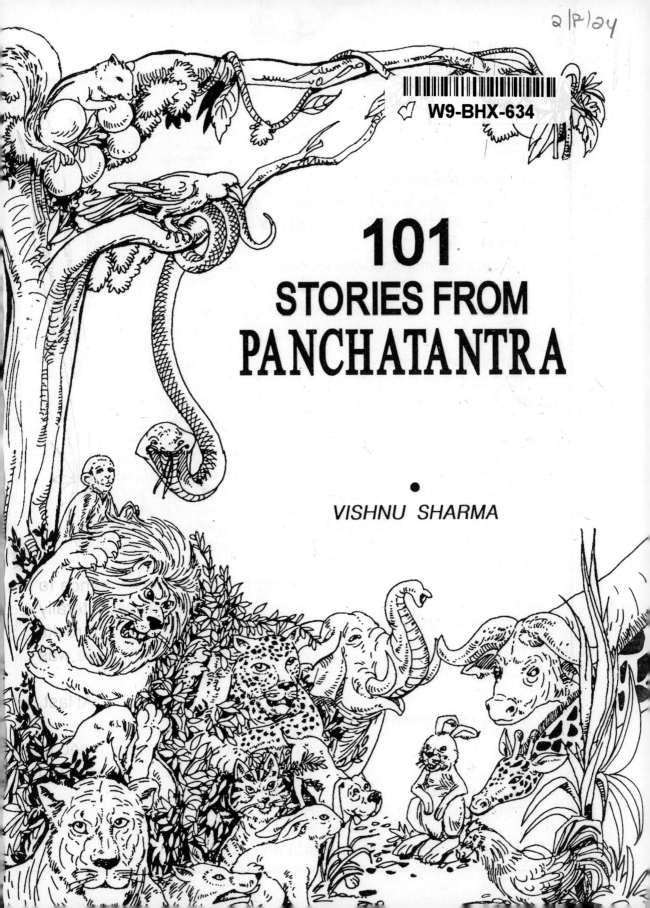

101
STORIES FROM
PANCHATANTRA

●

VISHNU SHARMA

Publishers :

Manoj Publications

761, Main Road, Burari, Delhi-110084

Phone : 27611116, 27611349, 27611546

Mobile : 9868112194

E-mail : info@manojpublications.com

(For online shopping visit our website)

Website : www.manojpublications.com

Showroom :

Manoj Publications

1583-84, Dariba Kalan, Chandni Chowk, Delhi-110006

Phone : 23262174, 23268216, Mobile : 9818753569

ISBN : 978-81-8133-462-6

Twenty First Edition : 2015

Printers :
Jai Maya Offset
Jhilmil Industrial Area, Delhi-110095

101 Stories from Panchatantra : Vishnu Sharma

TO THE READERS

Since time immemorial the man and the animals have been living together, separated only by the stretches of the forests.

It's the man who has always tresspassed upon the woods and killed or maimed the animals for his food or for the skin, making, as a result, many of the animals species extinct today, or to be seen only in zoos or in sanctuaries, far away from their natural habitat. It's the man who has killed the birds for his food or has caged them for his pleasure. The beasts have seldom attacked the man, except when in danger or driven out of their jungle habitat deprived of their natural shelter and prey. They on their part, have proved themselves, on more than one occasion, a loyal and faithful companion of the man, as pets.

The stories from *the Panchatantra* as composed by the great Indian author Pandit Vishnu Sharma ages ago, unfold many facets of man's greed, cruelty, treachery, unfaithfulness, jealousy, harshness and lust for power and pelf, through the fine depiction of animals' behaviour and their interaction with man and the resultant underlying message is very clear. The *Panchatantra* in its time element discusses the sciences of philosophy, politics, music, astronomy, human relationship in a very simple style and teaches us the theme of togetherness, love and compassion, selfless courage, community living, mutual understanding and attainment of knowledge.

It's also hightime, when we should learn to respect the sanctity of animal kingdom and stop killing them for pleasure or for profit. We should teach our children to love the beasts and birds as they love us, unprovoked.

A few other stories not necessarily from *the Panchatantra* have been included in the book for an added reading.

We hope that these and the stories from *the Panchatantra* as retold here shall make an interesting reading to both the young readers, as well as to adults, alike.

—*Publishers*

PANCHATANTRA

Long ago, in the south of India, there lived a king by the name of Amarshakti, who ruled over the kingdom, known as Mahilaropyam. The king himself was an erudite scholar and an accomplished fighter as well. He was loved by his courtiers and subjects alike. The king had three sons, but unfortunately no princely traits were visible in them. They showed no signs of worthiness or capability of ruling the kingdom after the death of the king. On the contrary, they were dull minded and were not interested in studying or learning any other art or skill. This thought always tormented the king. So, one day, the king called all his ministers and courtiers to discuss this matter which was of great royal importance. He asked them to find ways and means to educate his unworthy sons. No minister or courtier, however, volunteered himself to impart education to the three sons of the king, despite being offered a lot of wealth by the king.

Ultimately, on the advice of a learned minister, the king invited a great Brahmin scholar, Pandit Vishnu Sharma, who accepted the challenge of educating the three foolish princes in 'Nitishastra' and that too within a period of six months. Pandit Vishnu Sharma also told the king that his services as a teacher would be free and that he desired neither wealth nor any part of the kingdom in return, as his remuneration as announced by the king.

Having decided upon this, the king expressed his gratefulness to the great Brahmin scholar and handed over his three sons to him, who after taking the princes to his hermitage (Ashram) began to recite to them some of his specially composed fables. These were interesting stories about animals and birds with a moral theme. These stories were labelled as *'Panchatantra'*. 'Panch' means five and 'Tantra' means the science of wise conduct in life, further elaborated by teachings of how to develop confidence, understand people, choose good friends, acquire wisdom and face the challenges in one's life. An old saying of the *'Panchatantra'* goes—'a man well versed in this science shall always achieve glory in his life.'

The Panchatantra is probably one of the few Indian classics, originally written in Sanskrit by the great Hindu scholar Pandit Vishnu Sharma at the age of 80 around 550 A.D. (or even earlier), which has been translated into more than 50 languages of the world. The story, as it goes back to the ancient times, depicts Hakim Burzoe, the royal physician of Persia (today's Iran) who came to India in search of 'Sanjeevini' herb to cure his ailing king and having failed to find such a herb he, ultimately, on the advice of an Indian scholar, came upon the famous treatise, *the Panchatantra* which, he was told, had a mystical healing effect, if read out loud to the ailing person.

So, the royal physician carried a copy of this wonderful treatise with him to Iran and there, he, after translating it into Pahlavi language, began to recite it to his ailing king, who remarkably got fully cured within a short period. This was, the beginning of the popularity of the *Panchatantra* in foreign countries like Arabia, Greece and then finally in Europe. Its Arabic translation appeared in the 8th century A.D. captioned 'Kalilah Diyanah Kartak Damnak', which even today is quite popular amongst the readers. The Greek and Russian translation of *the Panchatantra* appeared in the 11th century A.D. With the translation of this treatise into various European languages, *the Panchatantra* further climbed up the chart of its popularity. In 1251 A.D., it was translated into old Spanish language. In 1260 A.D. a few scholars of Italy translated the *Panchatantra* into Latin which, as a result proved a forerunner of its German translation in the year 1480. Later its translated version appeared in Italy in 1552. Its another successful translation was done by Sir Thomas North in 1570. The book ran its second edition in 1601. Thereafter, *the Panchatantra*, when translated into French, proved a craze for French book lovers and paved the way for its further publications in Nepali, Chinese and Japanese languages.

With regard to its publication in Hindi, it is believed that its translation into our national language appeared much later in the country.

However, despite all the uncertainties regarding the exact date of its origin, *the Panchatantra,* no doubt, is still treated as a great Indian philosophical treatise all over the world.

CONTENTS

1. THE BULLOCK AND THE LION

ONCE upon a time, a village merchant named Vardhmanaka, was going to Mathura town on his bullock cart. Two bullocks—Sanjeevaka and Nandaka were pulling the bullock cart.

While the merchant's cart was moving along the bank of the river Yamuna, Sanjeevaka, all of a sudden, stepped into a swampy spot. He tried to come out of the swamp, but couldn't succeed. The merchant too tried his level best to pull out Sanjeevaka from the swamp, but to no avail. Ultimately he had to leave Sanjeevaka there and proceed on with his onward journey.

Sanjeevaka thought sadly, "How I have served my master so loyally throughout my life and how my master has repaid my loyalty."

Now, Sanjeevaka was left to his fate. The only alternative he had— either resign to fate and die in the swamp or fight till the end. Sanjeevaka gathered up courage. He began applying his enormous muscle power. There is a saying—'God helps those who help themselves.' At last after great effort, he managed to wriggle his way out of the swamp.

Now, as he had nowhere to go and he didn't want to return to his master's house, he started moving along the banks of the river. He ate green grass in the nearby forest and drank fresh water from the river. Soon he became healthy and stout. He started bellowing like a lion. His thunder like bellowing could be heard miles away.

Once, king lion whose name was Pingalaka, came to the river to drink water. Suddenly, he heard thunder-like bellowing. He got frightened and ran away into his cave.

King lion had two jackals named Damnaka and Kartaka as his ministers. When Damnaka came to know that some kind of fear had overpowered his king, he asked him, "Your Majesty, tell me who is he you are afraid of? I'll bring him to you."

The lion, being the king was not ready to admit the fact, but after great hesitation, he told Damnaka the real cause of his fear. Damnaka assured king lion that he will find out the actual source of the thundering sound.

Soon Damnaka brought Sanjeevaka to the court of his king. "Your Majesty, this is the animal, who has been making the thundering sound.

He says that Lord Shiva has sent him to roam about in our kingdom."

King lion was very pleased to talk to Sanjeevaka. Soon he became friendly with him. He spent much of his time chatting with Sanjeevaka.

Gradually, king lion became very spiritual. He stopped killing his preys and even neglected his kingdom. This worried Damnaka and Kartaka and the other animals of the jungle.

Damnaka thought of a plan to solve the problem. One day, he went to king lion and said, "Your Majesty, Sanjeevaka has an evil eye on your kingdom. He wants to kill you and become the king himself."

And the next day, Damnaka went to Sanjeevaka and told him a different story. "King lion has a plan to kill you and distribute your flesh to all other animals of the jungle. Better you kill king lion with your pointed horns, before he kills you."

Sanjeevaka became very angry to hear Damnaka's words. He went to the court of king lion and started bellowing in a thundering tone. This annoyed king lion and he pounced upon Sanjeevaka with a thundering roar.

Both were strong. With the result they engaged themselves in a fierce fight. Sanjeevaka tried to kill king lion with his pointed horns, but in vain. King lion killed Sanjeevaka with his sharp claws and ate his flesh.

Though king lion killed Sanjeevaka but he felt very sad about it. After all, Sanjeevaka was once his friend. But since, Damnaka had convinced king lion that Sanjeevaka was a traitor, he had to act upon his advice. Later, he made Damnaka the chief minister of his kingdom.

Moral—*Never befriend a natural enemy.*

❑ ❑

2. THE TALKATIVE TORTOISE

ONCE upon a time, two geese by the names of Sankata and Vikata and a tortoise by the name of Kambugriva lived near a river. They were good friends. Once, due to drought in the region, all the rivers, lakes and ponds went dry. There was not a drop of water to drink for the birds and animals. They began to die of thirst.

The three friends talked among themselves to find a solution to this problem and go out in search of water. But despite their best efforts they could not find water anywhere around.

Having no alternative the three friends decided to go to some distant lake, full of water, to settle down there forever. But there was a problem in shifting to so distant a place. While it was easy for the geese to fly, it was difficult for the tortoise to cover that distance on foot.

So the tortoise put up a bright idea. He said, "Why not bring a strong stick? I will hold the stick in the middle with my teeth and you two hold both the ends of the stick in your beaks. In this manner, I can also travel with you."

Hearing the suggestion of the tortoise, the geese cautioned him, "It's a very good idea. We will do as you say. But you will have to be very careful. The problem with you is that you are very talkative. And if you open your mouth to say something, while we are flying, it will definitely prove to be detrimental to you. So, don't talk while you are dangling by the stick, otherwise you will lose your hold and go crashing down on the ground and die."

The tortoise understood the logic and promised not to open his mouth during the entire journey. So the geese held the stick ends in their beaks and the tortoise held the stick in the middle with his teeth and thus, they began their long journey.

They flew over hills, valleys, villages, forests and finally came over a town. While they were flying over the town, men, women and children came out of their houses to see this strange sight. The children began

shouting and clapping. The foolish tortoise forgot that he was hanging precariously. He became so curious to know the reason behind these clappings that he opened his mouth to ask his friends—"Friends, what is this all about?" But as soon as he opened his mouth to utter these words, he loosened his hold on the stick and fell down on the ground and died instantaneously.

Moral—*Always listen to friendly advices.*

◻ ◻

3. THE SAGE AND THE MOUSE

THERE lived a famous sage in a dense forest. Everyday, the animals of the forest came to him to listen to his spiritual preachings. They would gather around the meditating sage and the sage would tell them the good things of life.

There was also a little mouse living in the same forest. He too used to go to the sage daily to listen to his preachings.

One day, while he was roaming in the forest to collect berries for the sage, he was attacked by a big cat, who was watching him from behind the thick bushes.

The mouse was scared. He ran straight to the ashram of the sage. There he lay prostrate before the sage and narrated to him the whole story in a trembling voice. In the meantime, the cat also arrived there and requested the sage to allow him to take his prey.

The sage was in a fix. He thought for a moment and then with his divine powers transformed the mouse into a bigger cat.

Seeing a huge cat before him the other cat ran away.

Now the mouse was carefree. He began to roam about in the forest like a big cat. He meowed loudly to frighten other animals. He fought with other cats to take revenge on them and in this way killed many of them.

The mouse had hardly enjoyed a few carefree days of his life, when one day, a fox pounced upon him. This was a new problem. He had never taken into acount that there were yet bigger animals who could easily maul him and tear him into pieces. He ran for his life. He, somehow, saved himself from the fox and ran straight to the sage for help. The fox too was in his hot persuit. Soon both of them stood before the sage.

The sage seeing the plight of the mouse this time, transformed the mouse into a bigger fox. Seeing a big fox before him the other fox ran away.

The mouse became more carefree and began roaming about in the forest more freely with his newly acquired status of a big fox. But, his happiness was short-lived.

One day, while he was moving around in the forest freely, a tiger pounced upon him. The mouse, somehow, managed to save his life and as usual ran to take shelter in the ashram of the sage.

The sage, once again, took pity on the mouse and transformed him into a tiger.

Now, the mouse, after acquiring the status of a tiger, roamed fearlessly in the forest. He killed many animals in the forest unnecessarily.

After having been transformed into a tiger, the mouse had become all-powerful for the forest animals. He behaved like a king and commanded his subjects. But one thing always bothered his mind and kept him worried; and that was, the divine powers of the sage. "What, if, one day for some reason or the other, the sage becomes angry with me and brings me back to my original status," he would think worriedly. Ultimately, he decided something and one day, he came to the sage roaring loudly. He said to the sage, "I'm hungry. I want to eat you, so that I could enjoy all those divine powers, which you do. Allow me to kill you."

Hearing these words the sage became very angry. Sensing tiger's evil designs, he immediately transformed the tiger back into the mouse.

The worst had happened. Now the mouse realised his folly. He apologised to the saint for his evil actions and requested him to change him again into a tiger. But the sage drove the mouse away by beating him with a stick.

Moral—*However great one may become, one should never forget one's roots.*

❏ ❏

4. BEWARE OF MEAN FRIENDS

THERE in a deep jungle, lived a lion by the name of Madotkata. He had three selfish friends—a jackal, a crow and a wolf. They had become friendly with the lion, because he was the king of the forest. They were always at the service of the lion and obeyed him to meet their selfish ends.

Once, a camel got disorientated in the jungle while grazing and went astray. He tried hard to find his way out, but could not succeed.

In the meantime, these three friends of the lion saw the camel, wandering in a confused manner.

"He doesn't seem to come from our forest", said the jackal to his friends. "Let's kill and eat him."

"No", said the wolf. "It's a big animal. Let's go and inform our king, the lion."

101 Stories from Panchatantra—1

"Yes, this is a good idea", said the crow. "We can have our share of flesh after the king kills the camel."

Having decided upon this the three went to meet the lion.

"Your Majesty", said the jackal, "a camel from some other forest has entered into your kingdom without your permission. His body is full of delicious flesh. He may prove to be our best meal. Let's kill him".

Hearing the advice of his friends, the lion roared in anger and said, "What're you talking about? The camel has walked into my kingdom for the sake of his safety. We should give him shelter and not kill him. Go and bring him to me."

The three became very disheartened to hear the lion's words. But they were helpless. So having no alternative, they went to the camel and told him about the wishes of the lion who wanted to meet him and have dinner with him.

The camel was terribly frightened to learn the awkward proposal. Thinking that his last moment had arrived and soon he would be killed by the king of the forest, he resigned himself to the mercy of his fate and went to see the lion in his den.

However, the lion was very happy to see him. He talked to him sweetly and assured him of all the safety in the forest, so long as he stayed there. The camel was simply astonished and was very happy to hear the lion's words. He began living with the jackal, the wolf and the crow.

But once, bad luck struck the lion. One day, while he was hunting for food with his friends, he had a fight with a huge elephant. The fight was so fierce that all his three friends fled the spot in panic. The lion was badly wounded in the fight. Although, he killed the elephant, but he himself became incapable of hunting for his food. Day after day, he had to go without food. His friends too had to starve for days together as they depended entirely on the lion's prey for their food. But the camel grazed around happily.

One day the three friends—the jackal, the wolf and the crow approached the lion and said, "Your Majesty, you're becoming weak day after day. We can't see you in this pitiable condition. Why don't you kill the camel and eat him?"

"No", roared the lion, "he is our guest. We can't kill him. Don't make such suggestions to me in future."

But the jackal, the wolf and the crow had set their evil eyes on the camel. They met together once again and hatched a plan to kill the camel.

They went to the camel and said, "My dear friend, you know our king has had nothing to eat for the last so many days. He cannot go hunting due to his wounds and physical infirmity. Under these circumstances, it becomes our duty to sacrifice ourselves to save the life of our king. Come, let us go to our king and offer our bodies for his food."

Innocent camel didn't understand their plot. He nodded and consented in favour of their proposal.

All the four reached the den of the lion. The jackal said to the lion, "Your Majesty, despite our best of efforts, we couldn't find a prey."

First, the crow came forward and offered himself for the noble cause.

"So, you can eat me and assuage your hunger", said the crow to the lion.

"Your body is too small", said the jackal. "How can the king assuage his hunger by eating you?"

The jackal offered his own body to the lion for food. He said, "Your Majesty, I offer myself. It's my solemn duty to save your life."

"No", said the wolf, "you too are too small to assuage the hunger of our King. I offer myself for this noble task. Kill me and eat me, Your Majesty," he said lying prostrate before the lion.

But the lion didn't kill any of them.

The camel was standing nearby and watching all that was going on there. He also decided to go forward and fulfil the formality.

He stepped forward and said, "Your Majesty, why not me! You're my friend. A friend in need is a friend indeed. Please kill me and eat my flesh to assuage your hunger."

The lion liked the camel's idea. Since, the camel himself had offered his body for food, his conscience won't prick and the jackal had already told the lion about the intense desire of the camel to sacrifice himself for the welfare of the king. He immediately pounced upon the camel and tore him into pieces. The lion and his friends had a good and sumptuous meal for days together.

Moral—*Beware of people, who become friendly to fulfil their evil desires. They talk sweetly, but in reality, they are never trustworthy.*

5. UNITED WE STAND : DIVIDED WE FALL

In the middle of the jungle there stood a big peepal tree. A pair of sparrows lived on one of its branches. They had built a strong and comfortable nest and had two beautiful nestlings. They roamed the whole day in the jungle, collecting food to feed their young ones in the evening.

One day a huge elephant came to take rest under that big tree. He was hungry. So he tore off the branch on which the sparrows had built their nest. The branch fell on to the ground and the young ones of the birds were killed.

But, the elephant remained indifferent to all this and ate the leaves and the soft branches to his measure.

When the sparrows returned home in the evening, they found their young ones dead. They saw a big elephant lying under the tree and taking rest. Everything became crystal clear now. The elephant was the cause of the death of their loved young ones. The mother sparrow was grief-stricken. She began wailing over the loss of her nestlings.

Seeing her weeping bitterly, a woodpecker, who lived in a nearby tree, came to her to know the reason of her sorrow. The sparrows narrated the whole story. They expressed their wish to take revenge upon the elephant, for his cruel act. They wanted to see him dead.

"You're right", said the woodpecker. "This elephant has no consideration for others. He might, one day, kill my young ones too. Come with me. There is a sweet honey bee around here who's my friend. She is very intelligent. She might be able to tell us how the cruel elephant can be killed."

Having decided upon this, they went to meet the sweet honey bee. They narrated the whole story to her and expressed their wish to revenge themselves on the rogue. The bee consoled them and said, "Don't worry. I've a plan to kill that elephant—Listen, first I'll go to the elephant and sing a song in his ears. The elephant will close his eyes to listen attentively to my melody and when I have hummed him to sleep, the Woodpecker would poke his long beak into the elephant's eyes. This will turn him blind. Once he is blinded our job will be easy. I will go and express my sympathies and tell him to pour a few drops of the extract of a particular plant in his eyes to cure them. The elephant will go to fetch that plant. There will be a huge pit full of water lying on his way to the plant. When the elephant goes to collect the plant he will fall into the pit. Since, he will not be able to come out of it, he will die."

Then, as planned, the honey bee sang a song into the ears of the elephant. The elephant closed his eyes to listen to the melody more intently, and the woodpecker, without losing a single moment, made

21

him blind by pecking at his eyes.

The cruel elephant shrieked with pain. He began crying—'Oh, I have lost my eyes. I cannot see anything. Is there anyone who can help me?'

Immediately, thereafter, the honey bee again flew to the elephant, who on the advice of the bee set out to fetch the miraculous plant. But in the way the blind elephant fell into the pit and died.

Thus, the cock and the hen sparrows avenged the untimely death of their young ones and by causing death to the cruel and foolish elephant, they saved many more lives of innocent creatures.

Moral—*United we stand : Divided we fall.*

❏ ❏

6. THE TRICK OF THE CROW

ONCE upon a time, there stood a huge peepal tree on the outskirts of a small village. In this tree there lived a pair of crows with their young ones. And at the root of the tree there lived a big black serpent in a deep hole. Every time the crows laid their eggs, the serpent crept up the tree and ate all the eggs and the young ones. With the result, the crows were never able to raise their young ones. This made the crows very sad. They didn't know how to get rid of the killer serpent.

One day, the crows went to a fox. The fox was their intimate friend.

"Hello dear friends, come in", said the fox seeing the crows at his door, "You two seem to be very sad. What's the matter?"

"The root cause of our problem is a black serpent. He is after us. He eats up our eggs and the young ones. Please help us get rid of this bloody serpent," said the female crow to the fox.

The fox too was shocked to hear this sad story. She promised to help the crows.

She thought for a few minutes and then laid out a plan before the crows.

"Listen carefully", said the fox, "you know where the king's palace is situated. You've also seen the queen taking bath in an open swimming pool, inside the palace. The queen, while taking bath always removes all her ornaments and keeps them on a tray kept by the side of the pool. While she is busy taking her bath, you two swoop down upon the tray and pick up two diamond ornaments from it. Drop them into the serpent's hole. The servants of the queen will come chasing you and finding the ornaments into the serpent's hole, they will first kill the serpent to save them from being bitten by it and then will take the ornaments out of the hole. Thus, the serpent will be killed and you too will be saved from all the troubles of killing it by yourself."

This was a very bright idea. The crows liked it. They flew to the king's palace. There they saw the queen taking bath in a swimming pool. She had removed her ornaments and kept them in a tray. The crows swooped down upon the tray, picked up two expensive diamond necklaces from it and flew towards the snake's hole. The guards ran after the crows brandishing their sticks and swords. They chased the crows and soon reached that big peepal tree, where the big black snake lived. They found the diamond necklaces, lying inside the serpent's hole. Afraid of the snake, they first killed the snake by sticks and swords and then took out the ornaments and returned to the palace.

The crows thanked the fox for his help and lived happily in the peepal tree, thereafter.

Moral—*Intelligence is greater than strength.*

7. THE LION AND THE HARE

THERE lived a lion by the name of Bhasuraka, in a dense jungle. He was very powerful, cruel and arrogant. He used to kill the animals of the jungle unnecessarily. He even killed the human beings, who travelled through the jungle. This became a cause of worry for all the animals. They discussed this problem among themselves and ultimately came upon a decision to hold a meeting with the lion and make an amicable settlement with him and put an end to this ongoing trauma.

So, one day, all the animals of the jungle assembled under a big tree. They also invited king lion to attend the meeting. In the meeting the animals said to king lion, "Your Majesty, we are happy that you are our king. We are all-the-more happy that you are presiding over the meeting." King lion thanked them and asked, "Why is it that we have gathered here?" All the animals began looking at each other. They had to muster enough courage to broach the topic. "Sir," said one of the animals, "Its natural that you kill us for food. But, killing more than what is required is a positive vice and unnecessary. If you go on killing the animals without any purpose, soon a day will come, when there will be no animals left in the jungle."

"So what do you want?" roared king lion.

"Your Majesty, we have already discussed the problem among ourselves and have come upon a solution. We have decided to send one animal a day to your den. You can kill and eat it. This will save you from the trouble of hunting and you will not have to kill a number of animals unnecessarily for your meals."

"Good," the lion roared back. "I agree to this proposal, but the animals must reach to me in time, otherwise, I'll kill all the animals of the jungle."

The animals agreed to this proposal. Everyday one animal walked into the lion's den to become his feast. The lion too was very happy to have his food right before him. He stopped hunting for his prey.

One day, it was the turn of a hare to go into the lion's den. The little hare was unwilling to go and become a meal of the lion, but the other animals forced him to go to the lion's den.

Having no alternative, the hare began thinking quickly. He thought of a plan. He began wandering around and made a deliberate delay, and reached the lion's den a little late than the lion's meal time. By now, the lion had already lost his patience and seeing the hare coming slowly, he became furious and demanded for an explanation.

"Your Majesty", the hare said with folded hands, "I am not to be blamed for that. I have come late because another lion began chasing me and wanted to eat me. He said that he too was the king of the jungle."

The king lion roared in great anger and said, "Impossible, there cannot exist another king in this jungle. Who is he? I'll kill him. Show me where he lives."

The lion and the hare set out to face the other lion. The hare took the lion to a deep well, full of water.

When they reached near the well, the hare said to the lion, "This is the place where he lives. He might be hiding inside."

The lion again roared in great anger; climbed up the puteal of the well and peeped in. He saw his own reflection in the water and thought that the other lion was challenging his authority. He lost his temper.

"I must kill him", said the lion unto himself and jumped into the well. He was soon drowned.

The hare was happy. He went back to other animals and narrated the whole story. All the animals took a sigh of relief and praised him for his cleverness. They all lived happily thereafter.

Moral—*Intelligence is superior to physical strength.*

8. THE LOUSE AND THE BED-BUG

THERE lived a white louse by the name of Mandarisarpini in the spacious bedroom of a mighty king. She used to live in the corner of the bedsheet spread over the king's beautiful bedstead. Everyday, when the king was fast asleep, the louse sipped his blood and crept back again into a corner of the bed-cover to hide herself.

One night, a bed-bug by the name of Agnimukha strolled into the bedroom of the king. The louse saw him and told him to get out since the whole of the bedroom was her territory only. But the bed-bug said to her cleverly, "Look, you ought to be a little courteous to your guests. I'm your guest tonight." The louse got carried away by the bed-bug's

27

sweet talks. She gave him shelter saying, "It's all right. You can stay here tonight. But, you will not bite the king to suck his blood."

"But I'm your guest. What will you give me to eat?" the clever bed-bug asked. "What better food you can serve me than the king's blood."

"Well!", replied the louse. "You can suck the king's blood silently. He must not get hurt in anyway."

"Agreed", said the clever bed-bug and waited for the king to arrive in the bedroom and sleep on the bed.

When the night fell, the king entered into his bedroom and slept on the bed.

The greedy bed-bug forgot all about his promises and bit the sleeping king hard to suck his blood.

"It's a royal blood", thought the bed-bug and continued sucking till the king felt a terrible itching in his skin. The king woke up and then ordered his servants to find the bed-bug and kill it.

But the bed-bug hid himself very cunningly into the joints of the bed-stead and thus escaped his detection. The servants of the king, instead, found the louse on the bedsheet. They caught her and killed her.

Moral—*Never trust the strangers.*

❏ ❏

9. THE HUNTER AND THE DOVES

THERE was a huge banyan tree standing on the outer boundaries of a village. All kinds of birds had their homes in this tree. Even the travellers would come and relax under its cool shade during the hot summer days.

Once, a fowler came to take a rest there. He also had a huge net with him. He set his net under the tree and strewed some grains of rice to lure the birds. A crow living in the tree saw it and cautioned his friends not to go down to eat the rice.

But at the same moment, a flock of doves came flying over the banyan tree. They saw grains of rice strewn around and without losing a moment, descended on the ground to eat the grains of rice. As soon as they started eating the rice, a huge net fell over them and they were all trapped. They tried everything to come out of the net, but in vain. They saw the fowler coming towards them. He was very happy to find a large number of doves trapped inside the net.

However, the king of doves was very intelligent and clever. He said to other doves, "We must do something immediately to free ourselves from the clutches of this fowler. I've an idea. We should all fly up together clutching the net in our beaks. We will decide our next course of action later. Now, come on friends, let's fly."

So each dove picked up a part of the huge net in his beak and they all flew up together. Seeing the birds flying along with the whole net, the fowler was surprised. He could never imagine this. He ran after the flying birds, shouting madly, but could not catch them. Soon the birds flew out of his sight.

When the king dove saw that the fowler had given up the chase, he said to his friends, "Now we all have to get out of this net. There lives a mouse on the nearby hillock. He is my friend. Let's go to him for his help."

All the doves flew on to meet the mouse. When the mouse heard the doves making noise in front of his hole, he got frightened and hid himself deeper into the hole. He came out only when he heard the king dove saying, "Friend, it's I, the king dove. We're in great difficulty. Please come out and help us."

Hearing the dove, his friend's voice, the mouse came out of his hole and saw the king dove and his friends trapped in the net.

"Oh!", said the mouse, "Who's done all this to you?"

The king dove narrated the whole story. The mouse immediately started nibbling at the net around the king dove. The king dove said, "No, my friend. First set my followers free. A king cannot keep his subjects in pain and enjoy the freedom for himself."

The mouse praised the king dove for his nobleness and nibbled at the portion of the net, which would set free the other doves first. And only at last, he freed the king dove.

All the doves were very grateful to the mouse. They thanked the mouse and then flew to their destination happily.

Moral—*Unity is strength.*

10. THE FAKE KING

THERE lived a jackal in a jungle. His name was Chandarava. One day, he hadn't eaten anything since morning and was so hungry that he wandered and wandered across the jungle, but couldn't find anything to eat. He thought it better to walk a little farther and find something to eat in some village. He reached a nearby small village. There on its outskirts he ate some food, but the quantity was not sufficient and he was still very hungry. Then he entered another village with the hope of getting some more food.

As soon as the jackal entered the village, a few dogs roaming there charged at him barking loudly. The jackal was terribly frightened. He began running through lanes in order to save himself from the dogs. Soon he saw a house. The door of the house was open. It was a washerman's house. 'This is the right place for me to hide', the jackal thought to himself and ran into the open door.

While trying to hide himself, the jackal slipped and fell into a tank full of blue colour, which the washerman had kept ready to dye the clothes.

Soon the barking of the dogs ceased. The jackal saw them going away. He came out of the tub. There was a big mirror fixed on a wall of a room. There was no one around. The jackal entered the room and saw his image in the mirror. He was surprised to see his colour. He looked blue. He came out of the house and ran back to the jungle.

When the animals of the jungle saw the blue jackal they were frightened. They had never seen such an animal. Even the lions and tigers were no exceptions. They too were scared of the seemingly strange animal.

The jackal was quick to realise the change in the behaviour of the other animals. He decided to take advantage of this funny situation.

"Dear friends", said the blue jackal, "don't be afraid of me. I'm your well-wisher. Lord Brahma has sent me to look after your well-being. He has appointed me as your king."

All the animals of the jungle developed unshakable faith in the blue jackal and accepted him as their king. They brought presents for him and obeyed his commands. The blue jackal appointed the lion as his commander-in-chief; the wolf was appointed the defence minister and the elephant the home minister.

Thus, the blue jackal began living in luxury with the lions and tigers also at his command. What to talk of the smaller animals? The tigers and leopards brought him delicious food everyday.

101 Stories from Panchatantra—2

The blue jackal now was ruling the jungle. He used to hold daily darbar. All the animals were like his servants. Even the lion hunted small animals and gave them to the blue jackal to eat.

Once, when the blue jackal was holding his famous darbar, he heard a pack of jackals howling outside his palace. Those jackals had come from some other jungle and were howling, singing and dancing. The blue jackal forgot that he was a king and not an ordinary jackal any more. Instinctively, he too began howling, singing and dancing. All the animals were surprised to see their king howling like a jackal. Soon the word spread around that their king was simply a jackal and not a representative of Lord Brahma. He had fooled the animals. All the animals, in a fit of rage, killed the blue jackal immediately.

Moral—*One cannot fool all the people all the time.*

❏ ❏

11. HELLO! CAVE

LONG ago, there lived a lion by the name of Kharanakhara. He had been trying to hunt for his prey for the last two days, but could not succeed due to his old age and physical infirmity. He was no longer strong to hunt for his food. He was quite dejected and disappointed. He thought that he would die of strarving. One day, while he was wandering in the jungle hopelessly, he came across a cave. 'There must be some animal who lives in this cave'; so thought the lion. 'I will hide myself inside it and wait for its occupant to enter. And as soon as the occupant enters the cave, I shall kill him and eat his flesh.' Thinking thus, the lion entered the cave and hid himself carefully.

After sometime, a fox came near the cave. The cave belonged to her. The fox was surprised to find the foot-marks of a lion pointing towards the cave. 'Some lion has stealthily entered my cave', he thought to himself. But to make sure of the presence of the lion inside the cave, the fox played upon a trick.

The fox stood at some distance from the cave to save himself in case of a sudden attack and shouted, "Hello cave! I've come back. Speak to me as you have been doing earlier. Why're you keeping silent, my dear cave? May I come in and occupy my residence?"

Hearing the fox calling the cave, the lion thought to himself, that the cave he was hiding in, must in reality be a talking cave. The cave might be keeping quiet because of his kingly presence inside. Therefore, if the

cave didn't answer to the fox's question, the fox might go away to occupy some other cave and thus, he would have to go without a meal once again.

Trying to be wise, the lion answered in a roaring voice on behalf of the cave, "I've not forgotten my practice of speaking to you when you come, my dear fox. Come in and be at home, please."

Thus, the clever fox confirmed the presence of the lion hiding in his cave and ran away without losing a single moment, saying, "Only a fool would believe that a cave speaks."

Moral—*Presence of mind is the best weapon to guard oneself in every sphere of life.*

❏ ❏

12. THE OLD GREEDY CRANE

THERE was an old crane, who lived by a lake. He was so old that he could not arrange for his food. The fish swam around him, but he was so weak that he could not catch them.

One day, he was very hungry. He hadn't had anything to eat for days together. In total dejection he sat on the bank of the lake and began weeping. A crab who was passing by, heard him crying and asked him for the reason.

All of a sudden, he hit upon an idea. He asked the crab to have patience and allow him some time to overcome his emotion. The crab consoled him and became silent. Meanwhile, the crane pretended to have overcome his emotions and began saying in a sad tone, "Perhaps, you are not aware of the future of the acquatic animals of this lake. They will soon die without water."

"What!" the crab exclaimed.

"Yes", the crane said. "A fortune teller has told me that very soon this lake will go dry and all the creatures living in it will die. This thought of impending doom has sunken my heart with grief." After a pause, the crane continued, "There is another lake at some distance from here. All the big creatures like crocodiles, tortoises, frogs etc. can travel upto that lake, but I am worried about those, who cannot travel by land, like fish. They will die without water. This is the reason why I am so sad. I want to help them."

All the creatures in the lake were dumbstruck to know the future of the lake but they became very happy to know that the crane was ready to help them.

"There is a big lake, full of water, a few miles away from here. I'll carry such helpless creatures on my back", said the crane, "and put them safely in the big lake."

Everyone in the lake agreed to this proposal. Now the crane started carrying one creature at a time, on his back. First, he started with fish and carried them on his back; but, instead of taking them to the big lake, he took them to a nearby hill and ate them.

And in this way, the crane ate a large number of fish everyday.

Within a few days, he regained his health and became stout.

One day, the crab said to the crane, "Friend, you seem to have forgotten me. I thought, I would be the first one to be carried to the big lake, but I have a feeling that I have been completely ignored."

"No, I haven't forgotten you", said the crane cunningly. He was tired of eating fish everyday. He wanted to have a change. So he said to the crab, "Come my friend. Sit on my back."

The crab gladly sat on the crane's back and the crane flew towards the big lake.

"How far is the lake now?" the crab asked. The crane thought that the crab was quite an innocent creature. He would never know his evil plans. So, he said angrily, "You fool, do you think I am your servant? There is no other lake around here. I made this plan in order to be able to eat you all. Now you too be prepared to die."

But the crab didn't loose his senses. He quickly grabbed the long neck of the crane with his sharp claws and told him to return to the old lake. He threatened to cut the crane's neck into two, if he didn't obey him.

The crane was left with no choice, but to return to the old lake. On reaching the lake the crab immediately jumped off the back of the crane. Then he told all the other creatures about the crane's misdeeds. This made the creatures very angry. They attacked the crane and killed him.

Moral—*Never be greedy.*

❑ ❑

13. THE SHEPHERD AND THE WOLF

THERE lived a shepherd in a village. He had many sheep. He took them out every morning for grazing. One day, his wife fell ill and he had to go to the city to purchase some medicines for his ailing wife. 'There will be no one to take care of the sheep', he thought to himself. Then he called his son and told him, "Ramu, I'm going to the city to purchase some medicines for your mother. It will take me two or three days to come back. So take care of the sheep. Save them from being attacked by the tigers and wolves. There are many wild animals in the nearby forest. They might kill our sheep."

Ramu listened to his father's advice carefully and the next day, he left for the nearby hillside with his flock of sheep. But Ramu was a mischievous boy. He was feeling lonely. So he wanted to have some fun. He stood on a high rock and began shouting "Wolf! wolf!, help."

The villagers heard Ramu crying for help. They ran towards the hillside to help the boy, carrying big sticks in their hands. When they reached there they found that there was no wolf. The sheep were grazing happily and the shepherd boy was playing on a flute.

"Where is the wolf?" the villagers asked the boy.

"There is no wolf here. I was joking," the boy said and laughed.

The villagers became very angry and returned to their work in the village.

Next day, the boy played the same trick. The villagers again reached there to help the boy. But when they came to know that the boy was lying, they felt highly annoyed and went back to the village cursing the boy.

But on the third day, a wolf really came there. The boy got frightened to see his red eyes. The wolf was huffing and growling. He began advancing towards the flock of sheep, gnashing his teeth and lolling his tongue. The boy lost his courage and began trembling with fear. He shouted, "Wolf, wolf, please help!" But to no avail.

This time no one came to help him. The villagers thought that Ramu was upto his old tricks. The wolf killed many sheep of Ramu. Ramu returned home weeping.

Moral—*People do not trust a liar.*

❏ ❏

14. THE KING COBRA AND THE ANTS

THERE lived a big king cobra in a dense forest. As usual, he fed on birds' eggs, lizards, frogs and other small creatures. The whole night he hunted the small creatures and when the day broke, he went into his hole to sleep. Gradually, he became fat. And his fat grew to such a measure that it became difficult for him to enter and come out of his hole without being scratched.

Ultimately, he decided to abandon his hole and selected a huge tree for his new home. But there was an ant hill at the root of the tree. It was impossible for king cobra to put up with the ants. So, he went to the ant hill and said, "I'm King Cobra, the king of this forest. I order all of you to go from this place and live somewhere else."

There were other animals, too, around. They began trembling with fear to see such a huge snake before them. They ran for their lives. But the ants paid no heed to his threats. Thousands of ants streamed out of the ant hill. Soon they were swarming all over the body of the king cobra, stinging and biting him. Thousands of thorny pricks all over his

body caused unbearable pain to him. The king cobra tried to keep the ants away, but in vain. He wriggled in pain and at last, died a painful death.

Moral—*Even the strong and mighty cannot face the small ones, when in a large number, at a time.*

15. THE BEAR AND GOLU AND MOLU

GOLU and Molu were fast friends. Golu was a lean and thin boy, whereas Molu was fat. People, in the village laughed at this combination. For a major period of the day, they would be seen together. Everyone admired their friendship. Once, they got an invitation from one of their friends, who had invited them to attend his sister's marriage. The marriage was to take place in a nearby village.

But in order to reach the village, one had to pass through a forest, which was full of wild animals like tigers and bears etc.

While walking through the forest, Golu and Molu saw a bear coming towards them. Both of them got frightened. Golu who was lean and skinny, ran towards a big tree and climbed on it. Poor Molu being fat could not run fast and climb up the tree. But he showed his presence of mind. He had heard that bears did not eat dead bodies. So he lay down still on the ground and held his breath for a while, feighning himself dead. The bear came near Molu growling. He sniffed at his face and body. He took Molu to be a dead body and went away.

When the bear had gone away, Golu climbed down the tree. He went to Molu and asked, "I saw the bear talking to you. What did he say to you, my friend?"

"Don't call me a friend", said Molu. "And that is what the bear also told me. He had said to me, 'Don't trust Golu. He is not your friend."

Golu was very ashamed. He felt sorry to have left his friend alone when in danger. Thus, their friendship ended for ever.

Moral—*A friend in need is a friend indeed.*

❏ ❏

16. THE MONKEY AND THE CROCODILE

Long, long ago, there lived a huge crocodile in the river Ganges. The river flowed through a dense jungle. On both sides of the river there stood tall jamun and other fruit trees. In one such tree there lived a big monkey by the name of Raktamukha. He ate fruits from the tree and

passed his days happily jumping from one tree to another. Sometimes, he climbed down the tree; took a bath in the river and rested for a while on its bank.

One day, the crocodile came out of the river and sat under the big jamun tree in which the monkey lived. The monkey who was sitting high on a branch saw the crocodile taking rest under the tree. He became very eager to talk to the crocodile and cultivate a friendship with him.

"Since you're taking rest under the tree", said the moneky, "you're my guest. It's my duty to offer you food."

The monkey gave jamuns and other fruits to the crocodile to eat. The crocodile ate them and thanked the monkey for his hospitality.

The monkey and the crocodile talked together for hours and soon they became friends. They developed such friendship that neither of the two was happy to miss each other's company even for a single day. Early since morning, the monkey would start looking for the crocodile, and the crocodile would also swim up to the jamun tree as early as possible. They would sit together, have a hearty chat and the monkey would offer him the delicious jamuns. This became their daily routine.

One day, the monkey gave some fruits to the crocodile for his wife, as well. The crocodile took the fruits happily to his wife and also narrated the whole story to her.

The next day, the crocodile's wife said to her husband, "Dear, if these fruits are so tasty, then the monkey who eats these fruits must be ten times more tasty. Why don't you bring the heart of this monkey for my meals?"

The crocodile was shocked to hear these words from his wife. He said, "Darling, the monkey is my friend. It would not be fair to take his heart away from him."

"That means, you don't love me", said the crocodile's wife and began to weep.

"Don't weep, dear", said the crocodile. "I'll bring the monkey's heart for you."

The crocodile swiftly swam to the other bank of the river and reached the tree where the monkey lived.

"My wife and I invite you to our home for a dinner. My wife is very angry with me for not having invited you earlier," the crocodile said in a sad tone.

"But how will I go with you?" asked the monkey. "I don't know how to swim."

"Don't worry", said the crocodile. "Just ride on my back. I'll take you to my house."

The monkey happily sat on the back of the crocodile and the crocodile started his journey in the water.

While in mid stream, the monkey became frightened to see the water all around him and asked the crocodile to swim at a slow speed so that he did not fall into the river.

The crocodile thought that he could reveal his real intentions to the monkey, since it was impossible for him to escape from the middle of the river. So he said to the monkey, "I am taking you to my home to please my wife. She wants to eat your heart. She says that since you eat tasty fruits day and night, your heart must be ten times more tasty than those fruits."

The monkey was taken aback to hear these words. He had never expected this type of a request from a friend. He kept his mental cool and said wittingly, "Very well friend. It would be my privilege to offer my heart to your charming wife. But alas! you didn't inform me earlier, otherwise, I'd have carried my heart with me. Which I usually keep in the hollow of the tree."

"Oh!" said the crocodile, "I didn't think of it earlier. Now we'll have to go back to the tree."

The crocodile turned and swam back to the bank of the river where the monkey lived.

Upon reaching the bank the monkey jumped off the crocodile's back and quickly climbed up his home tree.

The crocodile waited for hours together for the monkey to return carrying his heart.

When the crocodile realised that the monkey was taking too long searching for his heart, he called him from the ground and said, "Friend, I believe, you must have found your heart by now. Now, please come down. My wife must be waiting for us and getting worried."

But the monkey laughed and said sitting at the top of the tree, "My dear foolish friend. You've deceived me as a friend. Can any one take out his heart and keep that in a hollow. It was all a trick to save my life and teach a lesson to a treacherous friend like you. Now get lost."

The crocodile returned home with his head bent down.

Moral—*At times presence of mind pays well.*

17. THE FROG AND THE SERPENT

THERE lived a frog king by the name of Gangadatta, in a deep well. His subjects and other relatives too lived in the same well. The relatives had an evil eye on his throne and often created problems for the king frog. In order to disrupt the smooth working of the kingdom, and with a view to cause impediments, they hatched a plan with the connivance of a minister of the kingdom and soon there was a revolt against the king frog. The king frog somehow managed to subdue the revolt, but he was very unhappy. He took a vow to take a revenge and teach them the lesson of their life. One day, he came out of the well with the help of iron chains hanging on the walls of the well. He headed straight towards the hole of a big black serpent, which he had seen earlier.

Keeping himself at a considerably safe distance, king frog called out to the serpent. The serpent was surprised to hear a frog calling him. He came out of the hole.

"I wish to be your friend", said the king frog.

"But we are born enemies," replied the serpent. "How's it possible?"

"I will make it possible. I have a proposal," said king frog. He spoke to the serpent about his plan and told him that he was bent upon teaching his relatives a lesson. "I want to punish them. I will take you to the well and in the process you can eat them all."

"Is it a dry well?" asked the serpent.

"There is not much water in it", said the king frog. "However, you needn't worry. There is a nice hole in the wall of the well, a little above the water level. You can eat my relative frogs and retire into it to take rest."

"Okay, lead me to the well. I'll teach your relatives a lesson", said the serpent hissing loudly.

The king frog took the serpent to his well and said, "Here live my relatives and rebels. You can eat them all, but please spare my near and dear ones."

"All right," said the serpent and entered the well followed by the king frog. There he started eating the frogs, one by one, as and when pointed out by the king frog. Soon all the enemies of the king frog were

eaten up by the serpent.

Now it was the turn of the king frog and his family. The serpent said to the king frog, "As you see, I've finished all your relatives and rebels. I've eaten your disloyal minister also. Now I've nothing to eat except you and your family."

King frog realised his folly. He had befriended his enemy to achieve his own selfish ends and settle his score with his enemies. The king frog felt as if the god of death was in his hot persuit. He, somehow, managed to gather some courage and said to the serpent, "No problem. I'll visit some other wells and ponds and persuade the frogs living there to resettle themselves in this empty well. Once they are in here, you can feast on them with ease."

"That's, good", the serpent became happy. "Do it soon. I'm hungry."

Both the king frog and his wife came out of the well and took to their heels, never to return to the same well again.

Moral—*Never look to an enemy for help.*

❑ ❑

18. THE BRAHMIN AND THE THREE THUGS

LONG, long ago, there lived a Brahmin in a small village. His name was Mitra Sharma. Once his father told him to sacrifice a goat according to some ancient Hindu rites. He asked him to visit the cattle fair in a nearby village and purchase a healthy goat for that purpose.

The Brahmin visited the cattle fair and bought a healthy and fat goat. He slung the goat over his shoulder and headed back for his home.

There were three thugs also roaming in the fair, with the sole intention of cheating the shopkeepers and other customers there. When they saw the Brahmin going back to his home with the goat, they thought of a plan to get the goat by employing the methods of thugery.

"This goat will make a delicious meal for all of us. Let's somehow get it." The three thugs discussed the matter amongst themselves. Then they separated from one another and took hiding positions at three different places on the path of the Brahmin.

47

As soon as the Brahmin reached a lonely spot, one of the thugs came out of his hiding place and said to the Brahmin in a surprised tone, "Sir, what's this? I don't understand why a pious man like you should carry a dog on his shoulders!"

The Brahmin was shocked to hear these words. He shouted back, "Can't you see? It's not a dog but a goat, you fool."

"I beg for your apology, sir. I told you what I saw. I am sorry if you don't believe it," said the thug and went away.

The Brahmin had hardly walked a hundred yards when another thug came out of his hiding place and said to the Brahmin, "Sir, why do you carry a dead calf on your shoulders? You seem to be a wise person. Such an act is sheer foolishness on your part."

"What!" the Brahmin shouted. "How do you mistake a living goat for a dead calf?"

"Sir," the second thug replied, "you seem to be highly mistaken in this respect yourself. Either you come from such a country where goats are not found, or you do it knowingly. I just told you what I saw. Thank you." The second thug went away laughing.

The Brahmin walked further. But again, he had hardly covered a little distance when the third thug confronted him laughing.

"Sir, why do you carry a donkey on your shoulders? It makes you a laughing stock", said the thug and began to laugh again.

The Brahmin hearing the words of the third thug became highly worried. 'Is it really not a goat!' He began to think. "Is it some kind of a ghost!"

The Brahmin got frightened. He thought to himself that the animal he was carrying on his shoulders might certainly be some sort of a ghost, because, it transformed itself from goat into a dog, from dog into a dead calf and from dead calf into a donkey.

The Brahmin was then terrified to such an extent that he flung the goat on to the roadside and fled.

The thugs caught the goat and feasted on it happily.

Moral—*One should not be carried away by what others say.*

❑ ❑

19. THE KING AND THE PARROTS

ONCE a tribal king went to a jungle to hunt for birds. While hunting, he caught two parrots in his net. He was happy to catch the parrots as he could teach them to talk and then let his children play with the talking parrots.

But while the tribal king was returning home with his two parrots, one of the parrots escaped from the net and flew away. The tribal king chased the parrot, but the parrot disappeared in the sky.

The tribal king brought the other parrot home and taught it to speak like him. Soon the parrot learnt to talk like a tribal man.

The other parrot which had managed to escape, was caught by a sage. The sage liked the parrot and taught him to recite holy hymns.

The sage lived at one end of the jungle, while the tribal king lived at the other end.

One day, a king of a nearby kingdom came in the jungle riding on his horse back. When he approached the tribal king's house the tribal king's parrot shouted from inside the cage hanging outside the house, "Here comes someone. Catch this fellow and beat him thoroughly."

The king hearing the parrot speak in such a filthy manner, left that place and reached the other end of the jungle where the sage lived. The sage's parrot was also kept in a cage, which was hanging outside the sage's cottage.

As soon as the parrot saw the king approaching the cottage it said, "Welcome! Please come in and have a seat. What can I do for you? Have a glass of water. Eat some sweets."

After having welcomed him properly with all the etiquettes, the parrot called his master, "Guruji, here comes a guest on his horseback. Take him inside and offer him a seat. Serve him food."

The king was highly impressed with this intelligent talking parrot. He was quick to understand that good environment and training always yield a better result.

The tribal king's parrot spoke rudely, while the sage's parrot greeted him in a polite tone.

Moral—*A man is known by the company he keeps.*

20. THE REVENGE OF THE ELEPHANT

Long, long ago, there lived a big elephant in a small town. The elephant was of a religious nature and used to perform puja in front of a temple. Despite his enormous physique, he was a very loving creature. People loved him and offered him delicious fruits to eat.

While going to temple, the elephant had to pass through a busy market place. There a florist would give him a marigold garland everyday, while a fruit seller would offer him fruits. The elephant was very grateful to both of them for these presents. The people in the market place would gather around the elephant and show their affections by patting him gently. They had a lot of respect in their hearts for him.

One day, the florist thought of playing a little joke on the elephant. When the elephant arrived at his shop the next day, as usual, he, instead of offering him a garland, pricked his trunk with a needle, which he used for making garlands.

The elephant writhed in pain and sat on the ground. Some people gathered around him and began to laugh.

This made the elephant very angry with the florist. That day he didn't visit the temple, but instead, went to a nearby dirty pond. At the pond he collected some dirty water in his long trunk and came back to the florist's shop. There he emptied his trunk by spewing dirty water upon the florist and the garlands and flowers kept in the shop. The flowers and garlands became dirty and could not be sold in the market. Thus the florist had to suffer a heavy loss for his mischief.

Moral—*Tit for tat.*

❑ ❑

21. THE LITTLE MICE AND THE BIG ELEPHANTS

ONCE upon a time a village was devastated by a strong earthquake. Damaged houses and roads could be seen everywhere. The village was, as a matter of fact, in a total ruin. The villagers had abandoned their houses and had settled in a nearby village. Finding the place totally devoid of residents, the mice began to live in the ruined houses. Soon their number grew into thousands and millions.

There was also a big lake situated near the ruined village. A herd of elephants used to visit the lake for drinking water. The herd had no other way but to pass through the ruins of the village to reach the lake. While on their way, the elephants trampled hundreds of mice daily under their heavy feet. This made all the mice very sad. Many of them were killed while a large number of them were maimed.

In order to find a solution to this problem, the mice held a meeting. In the meeting, it was decided that a request should be made to the king of elephants to this effect. The king of mice met the king of elephants and said to him, "Your Majesty, we live in the ruins of the village, but everytime your herd crosses the village, thousands of my subjects get trampled under the massive feet of your herd. Kindly change your route. If you do so, we promise to help you in the hour of your need."

Hearing this the king of elephants laughed. "You rats are so tiny to be of any help to giants like us. But in any case, we would do a favour to all of you by changing our route to reach the lake and to make you more safe." The king of mice thanked the king elephant and returned home.

After sometime, the king of a nearby kingdom thought of increasing the number of elephants in his army. He ordered his soldiers to catch more elephants for this purpose.

The king's soldiers saw this herd and put a strong net around the elephants. The elephants got trapped. They struggled hard to free themselves, but in vain.

Suddenly, the king of elephants recollected the promise of the king of mice, who had earlier talked about helping the elephants when needed. So he trumpeted loudly to call the king of mice. The king of mice hearing the voice of the king of elephants immediately rushed along with his followers to rescue the herd. There he found the elephants trapped in a thick net.

The mice set themselves on the task. They bit off the thick net at thousands of spots making it loose. The elephants broke the loose net and freed themselves.

They thanked the mice for their great help and extended their hands of friendship to them forever.

Moral—Sometimes a weak looking person may prove stronger than others.

❏ ❏

22. THE LION AND THE WOODCUTTER

THERE lived a lion in a dense forest. He had two good friends, a crow and a jackal. The lion hunted the whole day for his prey. And after assuaging his hunger, he gave the remaining food to his friends. The jackal and the crow were very happy to eat free food. They ate their fill and lazed around since they did not have to exert themselves to earn their food.

In the same village, there lived a woodcutter and his wife. Both husband and wife went to the forest to collect wood and returned home after hours of hard work. When they returned, the woodcutter's wife cooked meals and they both ate sitting in front of their house.

Once the lion saw the woodcutter and his wife sitting outside their house and eating tasty meals. He could get the smell of the food from quite a distance. He went near them. The woodcutter and his wife, instead of running away from the spot, very courageously welcomed the lion and asked him to take a seat beside them. The lion was surprised. He sat beside the couple and happily ate the meals offered by the woodcutter. The lion was very pleased to see the hospitality extended by them and he was all-the-more pleased to eat and enjoy cooked meals. This was for the first time that he got the taste of cooked meals, otherwise he had always had raw meals in the past. While returning to the deep forest the lion thanked the woodcutter and his wife for the tasty food.

The woodcutter's wife said to the lion, "You're always welcome. Please do come everyday and share the food with us."

Once again the lion was astonished. This kind of behaviour was uncommon among them. The animals would never offer food to others; rather, they would snatch each other's food and injure each other in the process.

The lion bowed before them with respect and went away. He took his lunch the next day also with the woodcutter's family. Gradually, he forgot to hunt for his prey and became lazy.

This change in the lion's habits was a matter of worry for his friends, the jackal and the crow. In fact, his friends had to go hungry as they no longer got the left-overs of the lion's food. They decided to find the reason behind the change in his friend's attitude. So both of them decided to keep a watch on the lion's activities.

One day, they saw the lion sitting beside the woodcutter and his wife and having a good meal. They decided to meet the lion on the spot.

But as soon as the woodcutter and his wife saw the jackal and the crow, they climbed up a nearby tall tree.

Seeing them running away the lion asked surprisingly, "What's the matter? Why do you run away from me today. I won't harm you."

The woodcutter replied, "We're not afraid of you. It's actually your two friends who frighten us. We trust you, but not your cunning friends. We have known them and their habits for a long time. They may prove more dangerous than you."

The lion was very disheartened to listen to this. He warned his friends not to meet him again.

Moral—*Beware of cunning people.*

❏ ❏

23. THE FOOLISH MONKEY AND THE KING

Long, long ago, there lived a king, who was very fond of monkeys. One big monkey used to serve the king as his personal attendant. The king considered him to be as intelligent as a human being. When the king took rest in his bedroom, the monkey used to sit beside him like his personal bodyguard.

Once the king returned to his palace after many days. He had gone to a nearby forest for hunting animals and birds. Despite best arrangements by his ministers for his comfort in the forest, he had an uncomfortable life, if compared with the comforts that he was used to in his palace. So, he went to bed early. He told the monkey to keep a watch around and see that nobody disturbed him during his sleep. The monkey sat near king's bed with a naked sword in his hand and started guarding his master.

After sometime, the monkey heard a small fly buzzing around in the room. The fly soon came nearer and sat on the face of the sleeping king.

The monkey first tried to shoo away the fly, but it kept on hovering over the king's face. It sat on his nose again and again. Seeing this the monkey lost his temper. He decided to kill the fly. So, when the fly sat on the king's nose again, the monkey hit it with the sword. The fly flew

away, but the sword fell on king's neck and he was beheaded. He died then and there on his bed.

Moral—*A wise enemy is better than a foolish friend.*

❏ ❏

24. THE HERMIT AND THE JUMPING RAT

On the outskirts of a small village, there was a temple, in which, there lived a pundit. He used to perform pooja in the nearby villages. In the evening, after he had finished his meals, he would keep the remaining food, if any, into a bowl. He would hang the bowl upon a hook, which was attached to the ceiling by means of a string.

There, in the same temple, lived a fat rat. He was so fat that he didn't fear even the cats. He would come out of his hole during the night time and jump over to the hanging bowl and eat whatever food available in it. The next morning, when pundit would open the bowl, he would find it empty. This went on daily. The pundit became very sad. He didn't know how to drive the rat away from the temple.

Once a hermit from another village came to stay with the pundit. The pundit had no food to offer to his guest. He became embarrassed and talked about his problem with the hermit.

"Don't worry", said the hermit. "We must find the hole where the rat lives and destroy it. The rat must have stored a large quantity of food in the hole. It's this hoard's smell that gives strength to the rat to make high jumps and reach the food bowl."

So the pundit and the hermit together traced the rat's hole. They dug it up and destroyed the food stock stored there by the rat.

The rat became frustrated to see his food stock destroyed. He lost his vital energy to make high jumps. He had to go hungry now. He became weak due to hunger and left the temple in search of food. While he was running around in search of food a hungry cat spotted him. The cat pounced upon him and killed him.

Moral—*The wealth does give strength.*

❑ ❑

25. THE WISE CRAB

THERE stood two big banyan trees, side by side, in a dense forest. In fact, they were at such a short distance from each other that they formed one huge banyan tree. Thousands of cranes lived in this tree. In a deep hole in its trunk, there also lived a big black snake.

The snake used to climb up the tree to its branches and eat the baby cranes from their nests, when their parents were away in search of food.

This had become a daily routine. And the unfortunate cranes were the soft targets. Every evening, on return to their nests, the hapless cranes would find their nestlings missing, and they were so helpless that they could not do anything to get rid of the big black snake.

One day, a crab saw some cranes standing by the side of the lake and weeping bitterly. He asked them the reason of their grief. The cranes said, "There's a big black snake living in the banyan tree. Everyday he eats up our babies. We don't know how to get rid of him."

The crab thought to himself that the cranes too were crabs' enemies. They ate crabs' babies. Why not give the cranes an idea which not only would kill the snake but finish the cranes also.

So, the crab said, "Don't weep. I've an idea which will help kill the snake."

"Yes, please help us," requested the cranes.

"There is a big mongoose living at a little distance from the banyan trees. You put a few fish all along the path running from the mongoose's hole to the banyan tree. The mongoose will eat the fish one by one and then reach the snake's hole. Now you can yourself imagine, what will happen thereafter."

The cranes became very happy to get such a brilliant idea. They acted according to the plan.

Thereafter, the mongoose ate up all the fish put all along the path leading up to his home and then reached the banyan tree. There he found the snake in the hole. A fierce fighting took place between them and the mongoose killed the snake.

But instead of going back to his hole after killing the serpent , the mongoose further climbed up the tree and started eating the baby cranes, one by one. Soon the mongoose ate up all the baby cranes living in the banyan tree.

After eating a large number of baby cranes, the mongoose became very fat and lazy. One day, while he was sleeping on a branch of the tree, he slipped and fell on to the ground and died then and there.

Moral—*Never act hastily on your enemy's advice.*

❏ ❏

26. THE CROW AND THE MONKEY

LONG, long ago, there was a big banyan tree in a dense jungle. In this banyan tree, there lived a crow's family happily, with its nestlings. They had a beautiful and strong nest on a thick and sturdy branch of the tree.

There was also a huge monkey living in the banyan tree. He had no house of his own to live in. Sometimes, he would sleep on one branch and sometimes, on the other.

Once it started raining very heavily. The rain was accompanied with thunder and lightening. Strong cold winds blew. There was not an inch of space left on the ground which was not lashed by the rain. While the crow's family protected itself from the fury of the rain by taking shelter inside the nest, the monkey could not find any safe place for himself. He began to shiver badly with cold.

The crow seeing the monkey in such a pitiable condition said to him, "Poor fellow. Even though you are stout and healthy, you never built a house for yourself. Look at us. We have a beautiful and strong nest to protect ourselves from the fury of the rain and storm. Why don't you build a house for yourself, instead of wandering around aimlessly and shifting from one branch to the other in a lazy manner? God has given you two hands; make use of them."

The monkey, hearing the crow's words became very annoyed. He

said, "You foolish black crow, how dare you advise me, and teach me the do's and don'ts of my life. You have lost your sense of etiquettes. I must teach you, how to behave with seniors." Saying so, the monkey tore off a branch from the tree and began to beat at the crow's nest. Soon the nest was broken into pieces. The nestlings fell down upon the rain soaked ground and died. The crows somehow flew away and took shelter on some other branch. They wept bitterly over their young ones' death. They had no time even to repent for their good intentioned advice given to the monkey.

Moral—*It's better not to advise others in their personal matters.*

❏ ❏

27. THE MONKEYS AND THE RED BERRIES

LONG, long ago, there lived a troop of monkeys in a hilly region. When winter fell, the monkeys began to shiver with cold. They had no place to protect themselves. One of the monkeys suggested that they should go to the nearby village and take shelter in the houses of human beings till the winter lasted. His suggestion was accepted by all the monkeys. All of them shifted from the hilly region to an adjoining village.

But, next morning, when the villagers saw a big troop of monkeys, all of a sudden, jumping from branches to branches and on their roof-tops, they greeted them by pelting stones and showing sticks.

Thus, the monkeys, instead of getting shelter in the village, were compelled to retreat to the hilly region and face the chilly winds and the snowfalls once again.

Then, ultimately one of the monkeys thought of making a fire to warm up the surrounding. He had seen the villagers sitting around fire and warming up themselves. There were some red berry trees around. The monkeys mistook them for burning coals. They plucked those berries and placed them under a pile of dry sticks. They tried to make a fire by blowing into the pile. But there was no fire. The monkeys became sad.

There were also a few birds who lived in the same tree where the monkeys lived. Seeing the plight of the monkeys, one of the birds said to them, "What a fool you are, trying to make fire from those red fruits. Have the fruits ever made fire? Why don't all of you take shelter in the nearby cave?"

When the monkeys saw the birds advising them they became red with rage. One old monkey said, "You dare call us fools. Why do you poke your nose into our affairs?"

But the little bird kept on chirping and advising the monkeys. Then one huge monkey caught hold of the neck of that noisy bird and dashed it against the tree trunk. The bird died on the spot.

Moral—*It's no use advising idiots. Instead, it might create more troubles.*

28. THE MONKEY AND THE LOG

ONCE some monkeys were sitting in a tree. The tree was at such a place, where construction of a temple was going on.

A carpenter was sawing a huge log to cut it into two parts. Just then the bell rang for the lunch break. The carpenter pushed a wedge into the split portion of the half sawed log and went to take his lunch, along with other workers.

When the monkeys saw that there was nobody around, they

jumped down from the tree and came near the temple. They began to play with the tools lying there. One of the monkeys, who was very curious about all those things, went round the half sawed log. Then sat on top of it. He spread his legs on both sides of the log, whereas his tail dangled through the split portion.

Now the monkey started prying the wedge out of the log with his hands. Suddenly, the wedge came out. The split parts of the log firmly snapped shut together crushing the monkeys tail in between. The monkey cried in pain and jumped off the log, but his tail was cut off for ever.

Moral—*Look before you leap.*

29. THE STAG AND HIS ANTLERS

Once upon a time, there lived a stag in a dense forest. One day, he went to a nearby lake to quench his thirst. There he saw his reflection in the water and thought to himself; 'I've got beautiful antlers, but my legs are ugly. I can't understand, why God has given me such thin legs.'

Just then, he heard a lion roaring at a short distance. The stag knew that if he stayed there, the lion will kill him. So he started running. The lion too started chasing the stag.

The stag ran faster and faster and soon he outdistanced the lion. But alas! all of a sudden, the antlers of the stag got entangled with the overhanging branches of a tree. The stag struggled hard, but could not free his antlers from the branches. He thought to himself, 'My thin legs helped me get away from the danger, but my antlers proved dangerous for me.'

By that time the lion had already reached there. He pounced upon the stag and killed him.

Moral—*A beautiful thing might not be useful also.*

30. THE DHOBI'S DONKEY

ONCE upon a time, there lived a dhobi in a village. He had a donkey and a dog as his pets. The dog guarded his master's house and accompanied him wherever he went. The donkey used to carry the load of clothes. The dhobi loved his dog very much. And the dog, whenever, he saw his master, would bark a little and wag his tail. He would raise his front legs and put them on the chest of his master. And the dhobi would pat his dog in return, for his loving gesture.

This made the donkey jealous of the dog's fate. He cursed his ill-fate; 'What a bad luck I've. My master doesn't love me in spite of my putting in hard labour. Now, I must do what this dog does to please my master.'

So, the next time, when he saw his master coming, he ran towards him. He brayed a little and tried to wag his tail. He raised his front legs and put them on his master's body.

The dhobi got frightened to see his donkey's abnormal behaviour. He thought that the donkey might have gone crazy. So he picked up a lathi and beat up the donkey till it fell on the ground.

Moral—*Jealousy is harmful.*

31. THE FALCON AND THE CROW

THERE lived a big falcon on a high mountain rock. Down in the plains, there lived a black crow in a huge tree.

One day, the falcon swooped down upon a rabbit on the ground. The falcon caught hold of the rabbit in his talons and flew back to his nest on the mountain rock.

The black crow saw the falcon do this thrilling feat. He thought to perform the same feat himself.

'What a fun it was to watch the falcon pick up the rabbit from the ground! Now I'll myself do this.' The crow thought to himself and flew high in the sky. Then, he swooped down with great force upon a rabbit sitting on the ground. But his swoop was not correctly aimed at and instead of catching the rabbit, he dashed against a heavy rock. His neck broke and his head cracked. He died on the spot.

Moral—*Never imitate others in a foolish manner.*

32. THE WOLF AND THE CRANE

ONCE, there lived a greedy and cunning wolf in a dense forest. One day, while he was having his dinner, a bone got stuck into his throat. He tried hard to take it out, but couldn't succeed in his effort.

The wolf began whining with pain. The pain was unbearable. The wolf got worried and began thinking, "The pain will subside in due course. But, what will happen if the bone doesn't come out. I won't be able to eat anything. I will starve to death."

The wolf began thinking of some possible remedy to overcome the problem.

Suddenly he recalled that there was a crane who lived on the banks of a nearby lake. He immediately went to the crane and said, "My friend, I've a bone stuck deep into my throat. If you could please pull it out of

my throat with your long beak, I shall pay you suitably for your help and remain ever-grateful to you."

The crane saw his pitiable condition and agreed to help him. He put his long beak, and in the process, half of his neck also, deep into the throat of the wolf and pulled the bone out. The wolf was very happy to have the bone pulled out of his throat.

"Now pay me my fees, please," The crane requested.

"What fees?", said the wolf. "You put your head into my mouth and I let it out safely. That's enough of my kindness. Now get lost, otherwise, I'll kill you and eat your flesh."

Moral—*Be careful of the wicked people.*

❏ ❏

33. WHO WILL BELL THE CAT?

ONCE upon a time, there lived many mice in a grocer's shop. There in the shop, they ate delicious wheat and rice, pulses and nuts, bread and butter and biscuits. They grew fat day by day.

One day, the grocer thought about the heavy losses that he had to suffer because of the menace of the mice. This angered him so much, that the next day, he brought a big fat cat to his shop.

The big fat cat began to catch and kill the fat mice everyday.

The mice became worried. They called a meeting to discuss the problem.

"Let's get rid of this cruel fat cat," the leader of the mice said.

"But how?" the other mice asked.

All of them began to think. Then one mouse said, "We should tie a bell round the neck of the fat cat. So, whenever she would move towards us, the bell would ring and we will run into our holes immediately."

All the mice became very happy to hear this. They began dancing with joy. But their joy was short-lived. An old and experienced mouse interrupted their merry-making and shouted, "Fools, stop it and tell me, who'll bell the cat?"

No mouse had the answer to this big question.

Moral—*Making a plan is one thing, but executing it is something entirely different.*

34. THE PEACOCK AND THE FOX

ONCE a fox was wandering in a forest. He saw a beautiful peacock sitting on the branch of a tree at a considerable height: 'How can I have this peacock for my meal,' thought the fox to himself. He knew, he could not climb up the tree to kill the peacock.

Applying his stratagem, the fox said to the peacock, "How is it that you are sitting in the tree? Don't you know that it has been decided in a meeting of animals today that from now on animals and birds will not kill each other for food. Bigger fish will not eat smaller fish."

"That means the king lion, tigers and leopards shall start eating grass from today," said the peacock, outwitting the fox.

But, the fox wasn't ready to give up so easily. "This point needs clarification," said the fox cunningly. "Come down, we'll go together to our king and request him to clarify this point."

"We needn't go there," said the peacock. "I can see some of your friends coming towards this tree."

"Who are they?" the fox asked in surprise.

"Hounds," the peacock replied.

"Hounds!" the fox repeated the words in fear and sprang up on his feet to run away.

"Why do you run away? You have just told that all the animals and birds have become friends to each other," the peacock said laughing.

"But, perhaps the hounds might not have heard of this meeting," the fox replied and ran away into the deep forest.

Moral—*Presence of mind outwits cunningness.*

35. THE FOOLISH JACKAL

THERE lived two big bulls in a village. The village was situated near a thick forest. Once on some issue the bulls began fighting fiercely on the outskirts of the village. They would keep their horns locked with each other for hours together. Then, they would walk back a little and again run into each other dashing their heads together. They engaged themselves in such a fierce fighting that they badly injured themselves and soon blood started oozing from their heads. But they didn't stop fighting.

A jackal, who who had been watching this bloody fight throughout from behind the thick bushes, saw the blood of the bulls dropping on to the ground. He came out of the bushes to lick it.

Without a second thought, the jackal made his way between those two bulls and started licking the blood.

While he was still busy licking the blood happily, the bulls again retracted themselves to a few steps and then rammed fiercely into each other. They dashed their heads together. The poor jackal got crushed between their heads. His stomach burst with a loud noise and he died instantaneously.

Moral—*Never loose yours senses out of greed.*

36. THE DONKEY AND THE LEOPARD'S SKIN

THERE was a washerman. His name was Shuddhapata. He had a donkey. The donkey had an insatiable appetite for food, but was least interested in doing his master's work. And Shuddhapata was very poor. It was not possible for him to feed his always-hungry and lazy donkey. Therefore, as a result the donkey became lean and thin.

Once the washerman had to go to the town to purchase soap etc. for washing clothes. He had to pass through a jungle on his way to the town. While returning from the town, he found a leopard's skin in the jungle. He immediately thought of a plan to feed his lazy donkey.

When the night fell, he donned his donkey with the leopard's skin and drove him to the nearby fields. The farmers were frightened to see a leopard roaming in their fields and ran away. The donkey ate his fill and returned home in the early hours of morning. This continued for months together. Soon the donkey became fat and healthy. No farmer ever dared come near him. The donkey passed his days and nights happily.

One night, as the donkey was feeding itself in a neighbouring field, it heard another donkey braying in a nearby village. The donkey became very happy to hear it and instinctively started braying in reply, "Dheechoon, Dheechoon". Soon the farmers realised that the animal they were frightened of was not a leopard but a donkey. They became very angry. They came out of their houses with lathis in their hands and beat the donkey so badly that it died on the spot.

Moral—*You cannot fool all the people all the time.*

❑ ❑

37. THE JACKAL AND THE ARROW

ONCE a hunter was hunting in a forest. After sometime, he felt hungry. He saw a wild boar coming towards him. He shot an arrow at the boar. The arrow pierced the boar's neck and protruded at its back.

But the boar, before falling on the ground, killed the hunter with his pointed tusks. Soon the hunter and the boar both were lying dead at the same spot.

At the same time, a hungry jackal happened to pass through that place. He saw a man and an animal, both lying dead there. 'What a good luck I have? So much food to eat for days together', thought the jackal to himself. He began to think whose flesh to eat first—the man or the animal.

He decided to go slow at the eating, so that the food would last for a longer period.

The jackal decided first to lick the blood and eat a little flesh stuck round the tusks of the boar. But, as soon as, he put the pointed tip of the boar's tusks in his mouth it pierced his jaws and went through his head. The jackal died on the spot.

Moral—*Greed never pays.*

☐ ☐

38. THE BRAHMIN AND THE SNAKE

THERE lived a poor Brahmin in a village. His name was Haridatta. He had a small farm to till, but in spite of all his hard work nothing grew in his farm.

Once, after finishing his work in the farm he felt so much tired that he fell asleep under a tree. When he woke up, he saw a snake sitting outside a hole at a little distance from him. Seeing the Brahmin the snake hissed loudly. The Brahmin became frightened.

He thought to himself: 'It must be lord cobra who is highly annoyed with me, because I never offered him milk. This might also be the reason, why nothing grows in my farm. So, I must offer milk to lord cobra and pray to him.'

The Brahmin offered a bowl of milk to lord cobra and prayed to him for wealth and happiness.

After finishing the milk, lord cobra said to the Brahmin, "I'm pleased with you. Bring a bowl of milk for me daily." Then he crawled back into his hole.

When the Brahmin went to collect the empty bowl of milk, he was astonished to find a gold coin lying in it. The Brahmin became very happy to get that gold coin. He thought it to be a blessing from lord cobra. Thus, he offered a bowl of milk everyday to lord cobra and each day he collected a gold coin in return from the bowl. In this way, the Brahmin collected hundreds of gold coins. His barren field began yielding a lot of crops. His days had changed.

Soon the Brahmin became a rich man. He started a big business in the neighbouring town. But he continued tilling his farm, as before.

Once the Brahmin had to go to a distant town for purchasing seeds of fruit and vegetables. He told his son to look after lord cobra and offer him a bowl of milk everyday.

The Brahmin's son offered a bowl of milk to lord cobra everyday as instructed by his father. Lord cobra drank the milk and soon thereafter, a gold coin appeared in the bowl, as usual.

One day, the son of the Brahmin thought to himself: 'There must be a lot of gold coins in the stomach of lord cobra,' what a fool my father was to collect only one coin a day.'

The next day he kept a bowl of milk outside lord cobra's hole and waited at a distance with an axe in his hand.

As soon as lord cobra came out of his hole to drink the milk, the son of the Brahmin cut off the neck of lord cobra with his axe.

Lord Cobra died. The son of the Brahmin slit the stomach of lord cobra, but he could not find any gold coin inside it.

After a few days, when the Brahmin returned home, he found lord cobra dead. He said to his son, "Oh! my foolish son, why did you do this? You killed lord cobra. Now we won't get even a single gold coin. It is better, you get out of my sight.

Moral—*Unthoughtful actions have no value.*

❑ ❑

39. THE CLEVER JACKAL

ONCE upon a time, there lived a jackal in a dense forest. His name was Mahachaturaka. He was very clever. One day, while he was wandering in search of food, he came across a dead elephant. He wanted to eat its flesh, but his teeth were not strong enough to cut through the tough hide of the elephant. So, he waited patiently for someone to come around.

In the meantime, a lion came there. The jackal said to him, "Your Majesty, please have a taste of the elephant. I have been guarding it for you only."

"I eat only fresh animals, not the stale ones," said the lion and went on his way.

The jackal became happy. He had still the full dead body of the elephant intact in his possession.

Next, there came a tiger. The jackal became afraid. He thought to himself that the tiger might eat up the whole elephant. So, he said to the tiger, "A hunter has killed this elephant with a poisoned arrow. Whosoever eats its flesh would die due to food poisoning. I'm guarding it to save the life of others."

The tiger got frightened and soon disappeared into the dense forest.

As soon as the tiger went away there came two vulchers. They sat over the dead body of the elephant. The clever jackal did not want them to eat the elephant. So he said to them, "I've hunted this elephant and have sold its skin to two hunters. If they ever see you eating the elephant, they'll kill both of you."

The vulchers became frightened and immediately flew away. But the jackal still looked for someone who would cut the tough hide of the elephant to make it easy for him to eat its flesh.

At last, there came a leopard. The jackal knew that the leopard had a sharp teeth. He could cut through the elephant's hide. He said to him, "Friend, you seem to be hungry. Why not take a bite on the elephant. It has been killed by a lion. He has gone home to bring his family. When I see him arriving, I'll make a warning sign and then you can run away."

The leopard agreed. He immediately sat down to cut open the elephant's hide. As soon as the jackal saw that leopard had cut through the elephant's hide and was about to eat its flesh, he shouted, "There comes the lion."

The leopard sprang up on its feet and quickly disappeared into the forest.

The jackal happily enjoyed the flesh of the elephant for many days together.

Moral—*Cleverness has its own advantages.*

40. THE GOLDEN BIRD AND THE KING

Long, long ago, there lived a magic bird by the name of Sindhuka in a thick forest. It laid golden eggs.

Once a fowler came to the forest. While hunting, he came near the tree in which lived the magic bird. He saw the bird laying golden eggs. He caught the bird in his net and returned home. But he was afraid of keeping the bird in his captivity. He thought that the magic bird would lay him golden eggs. Soon he would be rich. The king might think that he became rich by stealing others' money. He might send him to jail. So it was better that he himself presented the magic bird to the king.

Thinking thus, the fowler presented the magic bird to the king. The king was very happy to have such a magic bird. He ordered his servants to take care of the bird, so that it laid more and more golden eggs.

But the attendants said to the king, "Your Majesty, this is all a hoax. How can a bird lay golden eggs?" This created doubts in the mind of the king. He ordered his attendants to release the bird in the woods.

The attendants, thereafter, released the bird in the woods.

The bird flew in the sky and thought to itself, "This seems to be a fool's kingdom. The fowler knew that I laid golden eggs, but he gifted me to the king. The king in turn gave me to the attendants to release me in the woods. The attendants too didn't ever believe in my magical qualities and spoke to the king against me. And the biggest fool of them was I, who landed into the fowler's net."

Moral—*Take a decision after verifying the facts.*

❏ ❏

41. THE GOLDEN BIRDS AND THE GOLDEN SWANS

ONCE upon a time there lived a mighty king in the state of Rajasthan. He had a beautiful palace in the 'city of lakes'. One such lake surrounded his palace with a beautiful garden around it. There were many golden swans living at this lake. These golden swans used to shed golden feathers everyday. The king collected all such feathers and kept them in his state treasury.

Once, a huge golden bird came flying to the lake. He perched on the branch of a tall tree standing near the lake. He liked the lake's sweet water very much and decided to make the lake his home. But the other swans didn't tolerate his presence there.

"Who're you?" the golden swans asked the golden bird. "What for have you come here? Better get out, otherwise, we'll beat you."

"Why? Is this not king's palace ground?" the golden bird asked.

"It was," the swans replied, "but, not now. We've bought this place from the king. Now even he can't enter the lake area without our permission. Do you understand? Now get out of this place."

The golden bird then flew to the palace garden and waited for the king to arrive to take a walk in the garden. Soon the king came there with his armed guards and began to take morning stroll in the garden.

The golden bird then flew to the king and said to him, "Your Majesty, I came to your beautiful kingdom from a foreign land. I wanted to settle here. But, the golden swans already living here drove me out of the lake. They are very arrogant. They say that they have bought the lake from you and now even you can't enter the lake without their permission. I advised them not to speak ill, but still they talk arrogantly."

Hearing this the king became very angry. He ordered his soldiers to go to the lake and kill all those arrogant golden swans, because they had spoken ill of him.

However an elderly swan guarding the lake saw the soldiers coming towards the lake with naked swords in their hands, He was quick to know what was going to happen. He called a gathering of golden swans and said to them, "Let's fly to some other lake. The king's soldiers are coming to kill us."

Acting upon his good advice, all the golden swans took to their wings, well before the king's soldiers arrived there to kill them.

It was a great loss for the king, for he believed a stranger blindly and ordered his soldiers to kill the golden swans. Now he would never get those golden feathers. The golden swans too had to abandon the beautiful royal lake because of their arrogant nature.

The king became so dejected to lose those golden swans that he asked the golden bird to find a different home for himself somewhere else.

Moral—*Never act hastily believing a stranger's words. It's also undesirable to be as arrogant as the golden swans were.*

❏ ❏

42. THE MOUSE AND THE BULL

ONCE upon a time there lived a big bull in a village. The village was situated near a lake. One day, when the bull felt thirsty, he started walking towards the lake.

There was a tiny mouse living in the same village. The mouse was sitting by the side of the lake and basking in the sun. The bull who was going to drink water from the lake stepped on the tail of the mouse. The mouse squeeked in pain. He looked at his tail. It was completely crushed. 'This foolish bull has crushed my tail. I'll bite this bull to death.' The mouse said to himself and jumped on to the bull's back and started biting him with his sharp teeth. The bull didn't feel any pain. He was rather unaware of the presence of a little mouse on his back.

After sometime the mouse was tired of biting the bull. Seeing no reaction, he jumped off the bull's back and stood before him blocking his way. The bull looked at the mouse and asked, "Why do you block my way? Get out of my path, otherwise, you'll be crushed."

"You've already done it," said the mouse angrily. He showed his tail to the bull and said, "I bit you all over your back. Didn't you feel any pain?."

The bull was surprised to listen to this. He laughed and replied, "Did I really stamp on your tail and did you really bite me all over my body? I never realised both. However I'm sorry, if it really happened?

The mouse was left speechless to hear the bull's answer. He thought to himself that it was quite useless to argue with that thick skinned animal. The mouse felt very much disgusted and went to his home crying in pain.

Moral—*It's no use arguing with a stupid person.*

❏ ❏

43. THE CUNNING SNAKE

THERE lived a brown snake by the name of Mandvishya near a pond. The pond was full of frogs—big and small. They were all leading a happy life under the good rule of their king frog. The big brown snake had become old and weak and could no more catch his prey easily for his meals. So he decided to play a ruse upon the frogs. One day, he went to the pond and lay there as if he was suffering from illness. After sometime, the king frog happened to come out of water. He saw the brown snake lying by the side of the pond in a pitiable condition. When he asked for the reason in a frightened tone, the snake said, "A week before, I bit the son of a pundit by mistake, because he had tried to kill me with a stick. He died immediately. Now the pundit has cursed me. According to his curse, I'll have to serve the frogs and have to eat whatever they offer me for food. So, I'm here to serve you."

The king frog and his ministers were delighted to hear this. Other frogs also gathered around the snake. Many of the minister frogs and the king frog too jumped on to the back of the brown snake to have a joy ride. The brown snake swam round the pond with all the frogs riding on his back.

The next day also the frogs rode over the entire length of the snake's back. The snake swam in the pond. Soon the king frog realised that the snake's movement had slowed down. When he asked for the reason, the brown snake said, "Your Majesty, due to constant swimming and non-availability of food, I've gone weak. I can't move any more now."

The king frog, thinking that in view of the snake's physical weakness, he might not be able to have joy rides in future, allowed the snake to eat a few frogs.

The brown snake, thus, started eating the frogs easily, one by one. One day, there were no frogs left in the pond, except the king frog. So the snake spoke to the king frog. "I can't remain hungry anymore. There are no frogs now left in the pond except you. So, please excuse me for eating you." And the brown snake attacked the frog with a lightening speed and ate him also.

Moral—*Never trust your enemy.*

❏ ❏

44. THE CAT, THE RAT AND THE HUNTER

ONCE upon a time, there lived an owl in a big banyan tree. A mouse, a cat and a mongoose also shared his neighbourhood. They all feared each other. The owl was scared of the cat. The mouse would be frightened to see the owl, the cat or the mongoose. The owl and the cat were the enemies of the mongoose. But despite all these problems, all of them continued living at the same place.

Once a hunter came under the banyan tree. He spread his snare there and waited at a distance for some animal to be trapped in. After sometime, the cat came there looking for the mouse. She stepped on the snare and got trapped. Seeing the cat in the net the mouse became happy and came out of his hole and began taking rounds of the trap in great joy.

Seeing the rat dancing outside his hole, the owl and the mongoose began to look at him with greedy eyes. The rat got frightened. 'The owl and the mongoose would surely kill me and eat me', thought the rat to himself. Also there were no chances for him to re-enter his hole, as both of his enemies were very near him.

The rat became nervous. He had to take a quick decision anyhow, lest he should be killed by the owl or the mongoose. At this dangerous stage, there was but one hope of survival, that he entered the trap and sat beside the cat and then request her to spare his life. If the cat did so, he would as a matter of his gratitude, nibble at the net at a hundred places to make it loose enough to set the cat free.

The rat took the chance of his life and ran into the trap beside the cat. The cat was about to pounce upon him, when he said to her, "Please don't kill me. If you spare my life, I'll bite off the trap at a number of places to set you free."

The cat agreed to the proposal of the rat and let him remain inside the net. Seeing the rat and the mouse together, the owl and the mongoose went away.

Then the mouse nibbled at the net at a hundred places. The cat came out of the trap and ran away into the dense forest. So did the mouse. He too ran into his hole.

The next day, when the cat wanted to meet the mouse, the mouse refused saying that enemies will be enemies; everything else like friendship between them will just be a temporary affair.

Moral—*Friendship with an enemy is a temporary affair.*

❏ ❏

45. THE FOX AND THE ELEPHANT

THERE lived a huge elephant in a dense jungle. He was cruel and arrogant by nature. He roamed freely in the jungle, pulling down small trees and branches. Those animals who lived in the trees were very much afraid of this elephant. When he pulled down the trees and tore off the branches, many a nests with eggs and nestlings came down crashing on the ground and got destroyed. His movement in the jungle created an all round havoc. Even the tigers and lions kept themselves at a safe distance from this rogue. In his ruthless march in the jungle, many holes of the foxes were trampled. This led to dissatisfaction among the foxes and among the other animals alike. Many of them wanted to kill the elephant. But this task was very difficult, because of his huge size.

"He is so huge", said the foxes amongst themselves. "It's nearly impossible to kill him."

Then a meeting of all the foxes was called. In the meeting this rather impossible task was assigned to a very cunning fox to perform. The fox, before executing his plan studied the elephant's behaviour for many days.

One day, the fox went to meet the elephant and said to him, "Your Highness. It's urgent to talk to you. It's a matter of life and death for us."

The elephant trumpeted at his highest pitch and asked, "Who're you and why do you want to see me?"

"Your Highness", said the fox. "I'm the representative of the whole of the animal community. We want to make you our supreme head—the king. Kindly accept our offer."

The elephant lifted his trunk with great pride and asked for details.

The fox further explained, "I've come to take you with me. The coronation ceremony will take place in the middle of the jungle, where thousands of animals have already gathered and are chanting holy mantras."

The elephant was very glad to hear this. He had always cherished a dream to become a king. He thought that the coronation ceremony will be a matter of pride to him. He readied himself hurriedly to accompany the fox to the deep jungle.

"Come, Your Highness," said the fox. "Follow me."

The fox led the elephant to some imaginary spot of ceremony. On their way, they had to walk through a swampy area by the side of a pond. The fox being light bodied, crossed the small swampy patch without any difficulty. The elephant too walked on it, but being heavily built, he got stuck into the swamp. The more he tried to come out of the swamp, the more he went deep into it. He became scared and called out the fox, "Dear friend. Please help me. I'm sinking in the mud. What'll happen to my coronation now. Call your other friends also to help me."

"I'm not going to save you", said the fox. "You deserved this treatment. You know, how cruel you have been to other animals all along. You pulled down branches of trees mercilessly, without caring for the eggs and for the lives of the nestlings. You knew everything, but remained indifferent. You trampled upon the burrows of the foxes. You saw our siblings being crushed under your heavy feet. You saw us crying, begging for mercy; but nothing bothered you. And now you are begging for your life? I am sorry to tell you that though, your coronation couldn't take place, but your cremation will definitely take place." And the fox left.

The elephant couldn't come out of the swamp and died there.

Moral—*Even a tyrant has to meet his doom.*

❏ ❏

46. THE GOLDEN GOAT

THERE lived a golden goat in a deep forest. He was as big as a pony and as strong as a bull. He had two pointed horns. His golden hair shone like burning flames in the bright sunlight. Even lions and tigers were afraid of facing this goat.

Once a lion saw the goat on the outskirts of a village, eating vegetable leaves in the garden of a farmer. The farmer seeing the goat in his garden beat him with sticks. The lion thought to himself, "How can a grass eating animal be stronger than I."

When the goat came out of the vegetable garden bleating after being beaten by the farmer, the lion pounced upon him. He killed the goat and ate it.

Moral—*Keep your eating habits and personal traits a secret.*

❏ ❏

47. WHEN THE LION CAME BACK TO LIFE

Long, long ago, there lived four friends in a village. Three of them were very learned, but they absolutely lacked in common sense. The fourth one, although not much learned, had a lot of common sense. He, at least, knew what was good and what was bad and was practical to quite an extent.

Once the three learned friends decided to travel to far off towns and cities in order to make their fortune. They were not ready to take their fourth friend with them, because he was not learned, but ultimately agreed to do so, considering that he was their childhood friend.

Soon the four friends set out on a long journey. They walked from one city to another, looking for an opportunity to amass wealth. Once, while they were passing through a dense forest, they came across a heap of bones lying under a tree.

One of the learned friends observed the bones and said, "Here is a fine opportunity to test our knowledge. These are the bones of a lion. Let's bring this lion back to life."

Then he assembled all the bones together to make it into a skeleton of a lion and chanted some mantras.

The second learned man chanted some other mantras and put skin, flesh and blood into the skeleton. Now it looked like a lion, but lifeless.

And the third learned man got up to do the final act of putting life into the lifeless body of the animal.

As he started chanting the mantras, the fourth friend shouted, "Stop! please don't do this. It might prove dangerous to bring this beast back to life."

"Shut up, you fool," said all the three friends. "What do you know in the field of learning and knowledge. Better you keep your mouth shut."

"Wait a minute please," said the fourth friend and quickly climbed up a nearby tall tree.

His three friends laughed. They put life into the lifeless body of the lion.

As soon as the huge lion came back to life, he roared loudly and killed all the three learned men. He ate their flesh and disappeared behind the thick bushes.

Moral—*Knowledge without common sense is useless.*

48. THE OLD WISE CROW

THERE stood a huge banyan tree on the outskirts of a small town. Thousands of crows lived in this tree. Not far from the banyan tree, there was a mountain cave. Thousands of owls lived in it.

The king of the owls accompanied by his soldiers used to hunt crows during the night. Soon thousands of crows were killed and eaten up by the owls. One of the main reasons for the killing of the crows at such a large scale was, that they were unable to see clearly during the night. And the owls, being nocturnal, could easily locate the crows sitting in the tree during night hours. And the unfortunate crows were defenceless; they couldn't fly away for the safety of their lives.

This kind of situation went on to such an extent, and the loss of lives of thousands of crows became so unbearable for the king of crows that one day he was compelled to call a meeting to discuss ways and means to combat the situation and bring an end to the continuing disaster.

After heated discussions and exchange of views and ideas, a plan was chalked out in the meeting, according to which a drama was to be enacted at a little distance from the owls' cave.

So, on the next day, the drama was staged and while enacting the drama, an old crow was 'thrashed' and 'beaten mercilessly' by the king of crows and his soldiers. The seemingly half dead old crow, with a goat's blood sprinkled all over his body was later picked up by the soldiers of the king owl. This was done on the advice of a senior minister in king owl's cabinet. This minister had told the king owl. "Your Majesty, this badly wounded crow had spoken in favour of us in his king's cabinet meeting, saying that ours was a more intelligent and superior race, better managed and strong, hence we deserved the right to be known and recognized as the king of birds. This led to the murderous attack on the poor fellow."

"We should help him recuperate from his wounds and injuries," said the king of owls. "After this, we'll utilise this old knowledgeable crow's talent in demolishing the kingdom of the crows."

The old crow soon found a favourable place in the owls kingdom. Many of the owl ministers were in his favour, except, one or two, who opposed the crow, saying that he was, after all, from the enemy's camp.

Despite this opposition from certain owl ministers, the crow continued to live in the owls' cave.

Lastly, it was the day time when the owls themselves were not able to see anything, due to sunlight, when the seemingly wounded and infirm crow piled up thousands of wooden logs at the mouth of the owls' cave and put fire into it. The devouring flames leapt up high and all the owls in the owls' kingdom, inside the cave, were burnt to ashes.

Moral—*Never trust your enemy. Don't allow him into your home.*

❏ ❏

49. THREE FISH AND THE FISHERMEN

LONG, long ago, there lived three fish with their families in a pond. Their names were Anagatavidhata, Pratyutpannamati and Yadbhavishya. Anagatavidhata was very practical. She always planned her actions in advance. Pratyutpannamati too was practical and always tendered good advices to her elder sister Anagatavidhata. Yadbhavishya, the youngest of them all, loved to laze around only. She didn't like to work at all.

One day, some fishermen came to the pond. One of them said, "This is the pond I was telling you about. There are many fish in this pond. Let's come here tomorrow and catch all of them."

Anagatavidhata overheard the fishermen's talk. She gathered all the fish in the pond and narrated to them what she had heard about. She said, "It's better that we move out of here to some other safer pond. Our life will, at least, be safe." Everybody agreed to this proposal including Pratyutpannamati. But Yadbhavishya said, "Why should we run like cowards from this pond. Let the fishermen come. We'll see to it together that we're not caught in the net. Besides, who knows the fishermen would really turn up here. After all, everyone has to die one day. So why be afraid of death."

But Anagatavidhata and Pratyutpannamati didn't agree with Yadbhavishya's ideas. They moved out to another pond with their families to live with their other near and dear ones.

The next morning, the fishermen came to the pond. They cast their net in the pond and trapped Yadbhavishya and her family alongwith a large number of other fish living in the pond.

Moral—*Always plan your future intelligently.*

❑ ❑

50. THE MICE THAT ATE BALANCE

ONCE upon a time, there lived a wealthy merchant named Jveernadhana, in a village. He ran a big business. His village was situated near a river. Once, due to heavy rains the river was flooded. One night, the whole village was submerged in neck deep wate The crop, houses and factories in the village were destroyed and hundreds of people and cattle perished in the flood.

The merchant had to suffer heavy losses in his business. He decided to shift to some other town to try his luck. His plan was to earn a lot of money and then come back to his native village to start his business again.

Jveernadhana had a heavy iron balance lying with him. It belonged to his ancestors. It was not possible for him to carry such a heavy thing along with him. So, before starting on his journey, he decided to keep this ancestral item with his friend Janak. He met Janak and requested him, "My friend, as you know, I'm leaving for some distant place to earn money, so that I could start my business once again when I come back. I have an old iron balance with me. Will you please keep it safe with you till I return?"

Janak readily agreed to his friend's request and said, "Don't worry, I'll keep it safe for you. You can take it back after you return home."

Jveernadhana thanked Janak for his helping attitude. He kept the iron balance with Janak and left for some other distant town.

A few years passed by. By this time, Jveernadhana had done good business and had earned a lot of money. He returned to his native village, and went to his friend Janak's house to meet him. Janak showed his happiness in meeting Jveernadhana. Both the friends talked together for hours. When it was time to leave, Jveernadhana asked his friend to return his iron balance. At this, Janak looked sad and said, "Friend, I am sorry to say that I don't have your balance with me anymore. There are a lot of mice in my house. They ate up your balance."

Jveernadhana was surprised to hear Janak's explanation. 'How can mice eat iron,' he thought to himself, but apparently he said something different, "Don't feel sorry, Janak. The mice have always proved a menace to everyone. Let us forget about it."

"Yes." Janak said. "This is the only way out." He was happy that Jveernadhana believed his words. In fact he had expected a lot of heated arguments in this respect.

While taking leave from his friend, Jveernadhana said to Janak,

"I'm going to temple to make an offering of laddoos. Could you please send your son with me. I would like to send some laddoos for you also. He would also look after my shoes outside the temple while I offer prayers inside."

Janak asked his son to go along with Jveernadhana. Then, Jveernadhana, instead, of taking Janak's son to temple, took him to a nearby hill and tied him with a big rock and came back home.

When Janak didn't see his son return, he asked Jveernadhana where his son was?

"I'm sorry," said Jveernadhana. "While your son was looking after my shoes outside the temple, a big vulture swooped down upon him and carried him away."

"What nonsense!" shouted Janak. "How can a vulture carry off a young boy?" But Jveernadhana repeatedly claimed that a vulture carried away Janak's son. The argument reached such a point that they began quarrelling with each other, using dirty words.

Ultimately the matter had to be taken to the court. The Judge listened to both the parties and ordered Jveernadhana to bring Janak's son to the court, otherwise, he would be sent to jail.

"My Lord", said Jveernadhana, "How can I, when a vulture has already carried away the boy."

"Shut up!" the judge reprimanded Jveernadhana. "How can a bird carry away a young boy in his talons?"

"It can, my lord," said Jveernadhana. "If mice can eat my iron balance, why can't a bird carry away a grown up boy." Then he narrated the whole story to the judge.

The judge then asked Janak to tell the truth. He warned him that if he didn't tell the truth he would be sent to prison. At last, Janak admitted his guilt. The judge ordered him to return the iron balance to Jveernadhana. He asked Jveernadhana to return the boy to Janak.

Moral—*Never try to deceive a friend.*

51. THE JACKAL AND THE DRUM

ONCE upon a time, in a jungle there lived a jackal by the name of Gomaya. One day, he was very hungry and was wandering in search of food. While wandering, he came across a battle field. There he saw a big drum lying under a tree. When the wind blew, a tender branch grown at the root of the tree struck the drum producing sound of a drum beat. The jackal examined the drum from all sides and then beat the drum with his front paws. The drum made a sound. Now the jackal thought that there might be some other small animal inside the drum and that would make a very tasty meal for him. But he found the top of the drum too tough to tear off.

The jackal thought of a plan and began to beat the drum with both his front paws. The sound of drumbeat filled the whole jungle. A leopard who was attracted towards the sound of the drum, came near it. The jackal said to the leopard, "Your Majesty, there is some animal hiding inside the drum. Since you have sharp claws and strong teeth, you can tear off the top of the drum and catch your prey inside the drum.

The leopard was himself hungry. So he hit the top of the drum with his heavy paws. The drum burst with a sound, but there was no animal inside. The drum was empty.

Seeing the empty drum, the leopard became very angry and said to the jackal, "You have wasted my time. There is no food inside the drum. So I will kill and eat you."

The leopard pounced upon the jackal and killed and ate him.

Moral—*Greed is always harmful.*

❑ ❑

52. THE LAPWINGS AND THE SEA

ONCE upon a time, there lived a lapwing and his wife on a sea-shore. When it was time for the lapwing's wife to lay eggs, she said to her husband. "I don't want to lay eggs here on the sea shore. The sea might eat up my eggs. Let us go to some pond or lake."

"Don't be foolish", said the lapwing. "Even our ancestors laid eggs here. Let the sea eat our eggs. I'll teach him a lesson, if he tries to do so."

The lapwing's wife laid eggs on the sea-shore and flew in the sky in search of food. But when she came back to the sea-shore, she was shocked to see all her eggs missing. She began to weep. When the lapwing came to know about it, he became red with rage. He called a meeting of all the birds and narrated to them the unjust and cruel exercise of power by the sea. Addressing all the other birds around him, he said, "Today the sea has swept away our eggs. Tomorrow it might be your turn."

The birds understood the logic and became highly upset over this incidence. They decided to meet their king, the eagle. The king eagle was infuriated to hear the story of the lapwing. He said to the birds, "Don't worry. I'll punish the sea for his misdeeds right now. I'll suck all its water and make it dry."

Lord Vishnu who was holding a conference in the heaven heard the outcry of the birds. He despatched his messenger to king eagle and told him to wait.

Then Lord Vishnu himself addressed the sea and put a condition before him that either he should return the lapwing's eggs or else he should be prepared to lose existence.

The sea god was frightened to hear Lord Vishnu's commands. He returned the eggs to the lapwing. He also promised that he will never wash away the birds' eggs lying on the sea-shore, in future.

Moral—*One should always fight against injustice.*

53. THE DONKEY AND THE CUNNING FOX

ONCE there lived a foolish donkey in a town. The town was situated near a forest. There, in the forest lived king lion and his minister, a cunning fox. Once, king lion was badly wounded in a fierce fighting with an elephant. He became unable to hunt for his prey. So he asked his minister, the cunning fox to bring some good meal for him. As the fox used to share the prey, which king lion hunted for his meals, he at once, set out to search for food.

While wandering here and there, the fox met a donkey. The donkey looked foolish, nervous and hungry. The fox asked him, "Hello! you seem to be new to this forest. Where do you actually come from?"

"I come from the nearby town", said the donkey. "My master, the dhobi makes me work all day, but doesn't feed me properly. So I've left my home to find a better place to live in and eat properly."

"I see", said the fox. "Don't worry. I'm a senior minister in this forest kingdom. Come with me to the king's palace. Our king needs a bodyguard, who has the experience of town life. You will live in the palace and eat a lot of green grass growing around it."

The donkey was very happy to listen to all this from the minister fox of the forest kingdom. He proceeded with him to the royal palace.

Seeing a donkey before him the king lion became highly impatient and pounced upon him immediately. But on account of constant hunger, the king lion had gone weak. He couldn't overpower the donkey. The donkey freed himself and ran for his life.

"Your Majesty," said the fox to king lion, "you shouldn't have acted in such a haste. You have scared your prey."

"I'm sorry," said king lion. "Try to bring him here once again."

The hungry fox went again to the donkey and said to him, "What a funny fellow you are. Why did you run away like that?"

"Why shouldn't I?" asked the donkey.

"My dear," said the fox, "you were being tested for your alertness as a royal bodyguard of the king. Thank god, you showed a quick reflex, otherwise, you would have been rejected for the job."

The donkey believed what the fox said and accompanied him once again to the palace. There at the palace the king lion was hiding behind the thick bushes. As soon as the donkey passed by the bushes, the lion pounced upon him and killed him instantly.

Just when the lion was about to begin eating the donkey, the fox said, "Your Majesty, you're going to have your meals after quite a few days. It's better you first take a bath and offer prayers."

"Hmm!" the king lion roared and said to the fox, "Stay here. I'll be back right now."

The lion went to take bath and offer his prayers. In the meantime, the fox ate the donkey's brain. When the king lion came back to eat his prey, he was surprised to see that the donkey's brain was missing.

"Where is this donkey's brain?" The king lion roared in great anger.

"The donkey's brain!" the fox expressed his surprise. "Your Majesty, you're fully aware that donkeys don't have a brain. Had that donkey ever had a brain, he would never have come with me to this palace for the second time."

"Yes," agreed king lion, "that's the point."

And he started eating happily the rest of the flesh of the dead donkey.

Moral—*Sometimes a cunning argument outwits normal intelligence.*

❏ ❏

54. THE MARRIAGE OF A SNAKE

THERE lived a Brahmin and his wife in a small village. The Brahmin couple had no children. They prayed day and night to God in order to be blessed with a child.

After years of praying, their wishes materialised and they were blessed with a child. But to everybody's shock, the child was a snake and not a normal human baby. The Brahmin couple was advised by their friends and relatives to get rid of the snake, as quickly as possible.

But the Brahmin's wife didn't listen to their suggestions and continued to look after the snake as her own baby.

Years passed by and the snake grew up bigger and bigger, till he reached the age of marriage. Now the Brahmin couple started looking for a suitable girl for their snake son.

The Brahmin went from village to village and town to town in search of a suitable girl, but all in vain. "How can a human being marry our snake child?" said the Brahmin to his wife. But his wife insisted for a suitable match for her son.

Having lost all the hopes from all sides, the Brahmin approached one of his old friends. He narrated his problem to his friend. "Oh! you should've told me about it earlier," said his friend. "I'm myself looking for a suitable match for my daughter. I shall be too happy to give her in marriage with your snake son."

The Brahmin couldn't believe his ears. But the marriage was solemnized despite protests. The girl was herself adamant to marry Brahmin's son, be it a snake, no matter.

After marriage the newly married couple—the girl and the snake—started to live like an ideal wife and husband. The girl looked after her husband's comforts dutifully. Her husband—the snake—slept beside his wife coiled in a basket.

One night, the snake crawled out of the basket into a room. After a few moments a young man came out of the room. He woke up the girl. The girl seeing a man in his room was about to scream when the young man said to her, "Don't be foolish. I'm your husband."

The girl didn't believe the young man. She said, "Show it to me before my eyes. I still don't believe it."

So the young man again slipped into the empty shell of the snake and then came out of it again transformed into a man. The girl became very happy to find such a husband. When the Brahmin and his wife came to know of this secret, they too became very happy.

One night, the Brahmin kept a watch over his son. As soon as his son came out of the snake's body transformed into a young man, the

Brahmin got hold of the snake's empty outer covering and threw it into the fire.

Then his son came to him and said, "Father, you've saved my life. Now, I can never be transformed into a snake. My outer covering has been destroyed in fire and with it has ended the long curse upon me."

So the Brahmin, his wife, son and daughter-in-law, all began to live a happy life, thereafter. The villagers too were happy to see them leading a normal and healthy life.

Moral—*After rains comes the sunshine.*

55. DEATH AND LORD INDRA'S PARROT

It was a meeting of all the gods in heaven. Lord Indra was also sitting on his thrown. His favourite parrot was perched on one of the arms of the throne. Lord Indra loved his parrot very much.

Soon, thereafter, the arrival of Lord of Death was announced. The next moment, entered the Lord of Death in the conference hall. The Lord of Death cast a glance at the parrot and smiled. Seeing him smiling, the parrot began trembling with fear, as it knew that the smile of Lord of Death must have some meaning and it could not be without reason. Seeing the parrot trembling with fear, the gods requested Lord of Death to spare parrot's life as it was very dear to Lord Indra.

"I've no authority in such matters," said Lord of Death. "You'll have to speak to Destiny in this respect."

So the request to spare the life of parrot was made to Destiny. But Destiny too expressed her inability to take a final decision with respect to the life and death of Lord Indra's parrot. Destiny said, "I'm afraid, you would have to approach Death, who will pass the final judgement in the matter."

The matter was, at last, referred to Death. And the moment Death looked at the parrot, it died. The gods became sad.

Lord of Death consoled them. "Death is the final Destiny of every living being. Be it a king or a beggar. There is no escape from this universal truth."

Moral—*Everyone who takes birth in this world has to die one day.*

❏❏

56. THE MONGOOSE AND THE BABY IN THE CRADLE

ONCE upon a time, there lived a poor Brahmin named Dev Sharma with his wife in a small village. The Brahmin used to perform puja in religious functions taking place in nearby villages. They had no children. They offered prayers to god for a child. At last, a son was born to them.

The Brahmin's wife had a mongoose as her pet. The mongoose was very playful. He used to guard the Brahmin's house and also looked after the baby, while it slept in the cradle.

Once, some people came to invite the Brahmin for performing puja in their house. The Brahmin was in a quandary. Should he go to perform puja or stay home to look after his baby? His wife had also gone to fetch water from the well situated on the outskirts of the village.

The Brahmin didn't want to leave the baby all alone in the house, even though the mongoose was sitting there beside the cradle like a baby sitter. He was in a state of perplexity. But at last he buckled under the pressure and went to the nearby village to conduct the religious ceremony, leaving the baby all alone in the house.

The mongoose still sat beside the cradle guarding the baby. Suddenly, he saw a big black snake crawling towards the cradle. Being a natural enemy of snakes and also having the responsibility of guarding the baby, he pounced upon the snake. After a fierce fighting with the snake the mongoose killed it.

But the mouth and paws of the mongoose were smeared with the snake's blood. The mongoose was happy that he had done his duty faithfully and had saved the baby from the snake. He ran to the main entrance of the house and sat there waiting for his master's wife to come back. He thought that she would be highly impressed with his performance and shall reward him suitably.

After sometime, the Brahmin's wife came along with the water pitcher on her head. She saw the paws and mouth of the mongoose smeared in blood.

She thought that the mongoose had killed her baby. In a fit of rage, she threw the heavy water pitcher on the head of the mongoose. The mongoose died on the spot.

The Brahmin's wife now went running inside the house. There she saw a big black snake lying dead. The baby was sleeping safe in the cradle. Now she realised that she was greatly mistaken, and the mongoose had, in fact, saved her child. She began repenting and weeping. She had killed her faithful pet without knowing what had really happened.

Moral—*One should avoid taking hasty decisions in sensitive matters.*

□ □

57. THE FOUR FRIENDS AND THE HUNTER

Long, long ago, there lived three friends in a jungle. They were—a deer, a crow and a mouse. They used to share their meals together.

One day, a turtle came to them and said, "I also want to join your company and become your friend. I'm all alone."

"You're most welcome," said the crow. "But what about your personal safety. There are many hunters around. They visit this jungle regularly. Suppose, a hunter comes, how will you save yourself?"

"That is the reason why I want to join your group," said the turtle .

No sooner had they talked about it than a hunter appeared on the scene. Seeing the hunter, the deer darted away; the crow flew in the sky and the mouse ran into a hole. The turtle tried to crawl away fast, but he was caught by the hunter. The hunter tied him up in the net. He was sad to lose the deer. But he thought, it was better to feast on the turtle rather than to go hungry.

The turtle's three friends became much worried to see his friend trapped by the hunter. They sat together to think of some plan to free his friend from the hunter's snare.

The crow then flew high up in the sky and spotted the hunter walking along the river bank. As per the plan the deer ran ahead of the hunter unnoticed and lay on the hunter's path as if dead.

The hunter saw the deer from a distance, lying on the ground. He was very happy to have found it again. "Now I'll have a good feast on it and sell its beautiful skin in the market," thought the hunter to himself. He put down the turtle on to the ground and ran to pick up the deer.

In the meantime, as planned, the rat gnawed through the net and freed the turtle. The turtle hurriedly crawled away into the river water.

Unaware of the plot of these friends, the hunter went to fetch the dear for its tasty flesh and beautiful skin. But, what he saw with his mouth agape was that, when he reached near, the deer suddenly sprang up to its feet and darted away in the jungle. Before he could understand anything, the deer had disappeared.

Dejected, the hunter turned back to collect the turtle he had left behind on the ground in the snare. But he was shocked to see the snare lying nibbled at and the turtle missing. For a moment, the hunter thought that he was dreaming. But the damaged snare lying on the ground was proof enough to confirm that he was very much awake and he was compelled to believe that some miracle had taken place.

The hunter got frightened on account of these happenings and ran out of the jungle.

The four friends once again started living happily.

Moral—*A friend in need is a friend indeed.*

❏ ❏

58. WHY THE OWLS BECAME ENEMIES OF THE CROWS

Long, long ago, all the birds of a jungle gathered to choose a new bird as their king. They were not happy with their king the Garuda, who they thought always enjoyed his time in the heaven and never cared for the birds. So, they thought it was better to choose a new bird as their king.

A heated discussion followed in the meeting and ultimately it was decided to make the owl the king of birds. The birds started making preparation for the coronation of the newly elected king.

Just then a crow flew in and raised an objection in the meeting. He said laughing, "What a bird you've chosen as your king. An ugly fellow. He also goes blind during the day. Moreover, owls are birds of prey. He might kill other birds for his meals rather than save them. Didn't peacocks and swans suit as your king?"

The crow's arguments made the birds think over their decision again. It was decided to choose the king on some other occasion and hence the coronation ceremony was postponed.

The owl chosen as the king of birds, still waited for his coronation as king. He realised all of a sudden that there was absolute quiet around him. No one was talking, nothing was happening. Since, it was day time, he couldn't see anything around him. He grew very impatient and a little suspicious also. At last, overcome by his curiosity and eagerness for his coronation as king, he enquired from one of his attendants, the reason behind the delay.

"Sir," his attendant said, "The coronation ceremony has been postponed. All the birds have decided to chose a new king. Now not even a single bird is here. They have all gone back to their respective places.

"Why?" the owl asked angrily.

"A crow put up arguments against us,—the owl family. He said we're ugly and killers."

The 'would be' king owl further lost his temper and said to the smiling crow who was still present there, "You've deprived me of the honour of becoming a king. So, from now on, we are sworn enemies of each other. Beware of us."

The crow realised his folly, but it was too late now.

Moral—_Think twice before you do or say anything._

❏ ❏

59. THE VISIT OF THE SWAN

ONCE there lived a swan by the side of a big lake. The lake was situated in the middle of a dense forest.

The swan was passing his days happily, until one day, an owl came there. He drank the water of the lake and started living there.

"This is an isolated place," said the swan to the owl. "Besides, the lake goes dry during the summer season. It is better that you go to some other place to live in."

But the owl stayed on there saying that he loved calm and quiet places; moreover, he liked the company of the swan.

"All right," replied the swan. "I too like your company. At least, there will be someone to talk to."

So, the owl lived happily in his company for months together. But, when the summer arrived in all its vigour and the lake really went dry in due course, the owl thought of returning home. He thanked the swan for the nice company given by him and said with a heavy heart, "Dear friend, I am leaving this place now, since the lake has gone dry and there is no water available here. I would like you too to come along with me; because you too can't live without water." "Thanks," said the sawn, "in fact there is a small river that flows half a mile away from here; I shall go and stay there. When the river also goes dry, I shall come and join you and once again we will be enjoying each other's loving company." "All right," said the owl, "there is a big river, a few miles away from here. And on its bank there is a big banyan tree; I live in it."

And then, once again, thanking the swan for his nice company and hospitality, the owl flew away.

The swan shifted to the small river and began living there.

After many days, when the small river also went dry and the swan felt lonely, he decided to meet the owl. One evening the swan flew and reached the banyan tree, the home of the owl. The owl was glad to receive the swan. He served tasty food and fresh water to his honoured guest.

The swan was tired because of his long journey. He took his meals and went to sleep early. The owl perched itself on the same branch, a little away from where the swan slept.

Just then a few travellers came to rest under the tree. The sun had set. It was near dark all around. The half moon shone in the sky. Seeing the travellers the owl hooted sharply. The travellers took it as a bad omen. One of the travellers shot an arrow at the owl. As the owl could see in the dark, he ducked the arrow and flitted away.

The arrow, instead, pierced the swan who was fast asleep at that time. The swan dropped dead on the ground.

Moral—*Make friends among people who are like you.*

❏ ❏

60. A POOR BRAHMIN'S DREAM

ONCE upon a time, there lived a poor Brahmin in a village. His name was Swabhavakripna. He was all alone in this world. He had no relatives or friends. He used to beg for his living. Whatever food he got as alms, he kept in an earthen pot and hung it beside his bed. Whenever he felt hungry he took out some food from the pot and ate it.

One night, the Brahmin lay on his bed and soon he was fast asleep. He began to dream—He was no longer a poor Brahmin. He wore good clothes. He was the owner of a shop. Hundreds of customers came to his shop. Soon he became richer than before. He purchased many buffaloes and cows. Very soon the buffaloes and cows had their young ones. Those young ones grew and became buffaloes and cows. The buffaloes and cows gave milk. He made a lot of butter and curd from the milk. He sold butter and curd in the market. Soon he became richer then ever before. He built a big house for himself. Then he married a beautiful girl. Soon they had their children. The children played around all day making noise. He then scolded them and asked them to keep quiet. But they won't listen. So he picked up a stick and ran after them.

The Brahmin began to move his legs rapidly while he was still asleep. In doing so, he hit the earthen pot with one of his legs which was full of food. The pot broke and the food contents were spilled all over the floor. The Brahmin woke up. He saw that he was still in the bed. All the edible items kept in the pot were scattered on the ground and became unfit for eating. All this happened because of his day dreaming.

Moral—*One should not build castles in the air.*

❑ ❑

61. THE BIRD WITH TWO HEADS

Long, long ago, there lived a strange bird in a huge banyan tree. The tree stood beside a river. The strange bird had two heads, but only one stomach.

Once, while the bird was flying high in the sky, he saw an apple shaped fruit lying on the bank of the river. The bird swooped down, picked up the fruit and began to eat it. This was the most delicious fruit the bird had ever eaten.

As the bird had two heads, the other head protested, "I'm your brother head. Why don't you let me also eat this tasty fruit?"

The first head of the bird replied, "Shut up. You know that we've only one stomach. Whichever head eats, the fruit will go to the same stomach. So it doesn't matter as to which head eats it. Moreover, I'm the one who found this fruit. So I've the first right to eat it."

Hearing this, the other head became silent. But this kind of selfishness on the part of the first head pinched him very much. One day, while flying, the other head spotted a tree bearing poisonous fruits. The other head immediately descended upon the tree and plucked a fruit from it.

"Please don't eat this poisonous fruit," cried the first head. "If you eat it, both of us will die, because we've a common stomach to digest it."

"Shut up!" shouted the other head. "Since I've plucked this fruit, I've every right to eat it."

The first head began to weep, but the other head didn't care. He wanted to take revenge. He ate the poisonous fruit. As a result both of them died.

Moral—*People living in a family should never quarrel among themselves.*

❏ ❏

62. THE DONKEY WHO SANG A SONG

ONCE upon a time, there lived a washerman in a village. He had a donkey by the name of Udhata. He used to carry loads of clothes to the river bank and back home everyday.

The donkey was not satisfied with the food, that was given to him by his master to eat. So he wandered into the nearby fields stealthily and ate the crops growing there.

Once, the donkey, while wandering around, happened to meet a fox. Soon, both of them became friends and began to wander together in search of delicious food.

One night, the donkey and the fox were eating water-melons in a field. The water-melons were so tasty, that the donkey ate in a large quantity. Having eaten to his appetite, the donkey became so happy that he was compelled by an intense desire to sing. He told the fox that he was in such a good mood that he had to express his happiness in a melodious tone. "Don't be a fool. If you sing, the people sleeping in and around this field will wake up and beat us black and blue with sticks," said the fox worriedly.

"You are a dull fellow", the donkey said hearing the words of fox. "Singing makes one happy and healthy. No matter what comes, I'll definitely sing a song."

The fox became worried to see the donkey adamant to sing a song in the midst of the field, while the owner was still sleeping only a little distance away.

Seeing his adamance, he said to the donkey, "Friend, wait a minute before you start. First, let me jump over to the other side of the fence for my safety."

Saying so the fox jumped over to the other side of the fence without losing a moment.

101 Stories from Panchatantra—7

The donkey began in his so-called melodious tone. Hearing, suddenly, a donkey braying in the field, the owner woke up from his sleep. He picked up his stick lying by his side and ran towards the donkey who was still braying happily. The owner of the field looked around and saw the loss caused by the donkey. He became very angry and beat him so ruthlessly that the donkey was physically incapacitated temporarily. He, somehow, managed to drag himself out of the field with great difficulty.

The fox looked at the donkey and said in a sympathetic tone, "I'm sorry to see you in this pitiable condition. I had already warned you, but you didn't listen to my advice."

The donkey too realised his folly and hung his head in shame.

Moral—*Think before you act.*

❑ ❑

63. THE RABBITS AND THE ELEPHANTS

ONCE upon a time, there lived a herd of elephants in a deep jungle. Their king was a huge elephant by the name of Chaturdanta. In the middle of this jungle, there was a big lake where all the animals went to drink water. Once it so happened, that it didn't rain for the whole year and the lakes went dry. The elephants, after a great deal of discussion, decided to move to the other forest, where there was a lake named Chandrasar. This lake was full of water and never went dry even if there were no rains.

And so, the elephants set out for the lake 'Chandrasar'. They felt very happy upon reaching the new lake. They bathed in the fresh water of the lake and also enjoyed playing and spewing water on each other by their trunks. After having bathed satisfactorily and quenched their thirst with the sweet water of the lake they came out of it and entered the deep forest.

But, there lived many rabbits in their burrows around the lake area. When the herd of elephants walked around they stamped the burrows with their heavy feet. Thus, many rabbits were either killed or were left physically handicapped.

So, in order to salvage the grave situation, the rabbits held a meeting and discussed this new calamity. At one point, they decided to shift from that dangerous place and live somewhere else. But a rabbit named Lambkarna advised them to exercise patience. He offered his services for the sake of all the other rabbits and said, "Don't worry friends. Just see, how I drive these elephants away from this forest."

The next day, Lambkarna sat on a high rock. The rock lay in the main path of the elephants, leading to the lake. When the elephants passed by the rock, the rabbit addressed the king of the elephants in a tough voice, "You're a cruel fellow. You've trampled many of my relatives and friends under your feet. I too am king of rabbits. I stay in the heaven with God Moon. God Moon is very much annoyed with you."

The king elephant was frightened to hear this. He said in a trembling voice, "Please take me to God Moon. I'll ask for his forgiveness."

"All right", said the clever rabbit. "See me tonight at the lake."

The king elephant, then, as told by the rabbit, reached the lake at night. The king rabbit and the king elephant both stood near the edge of the lake. It was a silent and moonlit night. Mild breeze was blowing. The rabbit asked the elephant to look carefully into the water of the lake.

As soon as the king elephant looked into the lake, he saw the reflection of half moon in the lake's water. Just then a mild breeze blew and the reflection of the moon in the water became wavy.

Pointing to the wavy reflection of the moon, the king rabbit said, "Look for yourself, how annoyed God Moon is with you. Better you ask for his mercy, otherwise, he might curse you to death."

The king elephant became more and more frightened. He promised God Moon not to ever visit the lake with his friends.

The rabbits lived happily, thereafter.

❑ ❑

64. THE CUNNING JUDGE

Once upon a time, there lived a sparrow in a tree. He was very happy to have a beautiful and comfortable nest of his own in the tree. The sparrow used to fly to far off places to pick at grains from so many fields, full of crops. At the sun set he would return to his perch.

One day, the sparrow ate his fill, but could not return to his nest, because of the heavy rains which continued for the whole night. The sparrow had to spend the whole night in a big banyan tree a little distance away from home.

The next morning, when the rain stopped and the sky became clear, the sparrow returned to his tree. He was astonished to find a rabbit occupying his beautiful and comfortable nest.

The sparrow lost his temper and spoke to the rabbit, "It's my home you're sitting in. Please quit this place at once."

"Don't talk like fools," replied the rabbit. "Trees, rivers and lakes don't belong to anyone. Places like these are yours only so long as you are living in. If someone else occupies it in your absence, it belongs to the new occupant. So go away and don't disturb me anymore."

But the sparrow was not satisfied with this illogical reply. He said, "Let's ask a person of wisdom and only then our case will be settled.

At a distance from the tree, there lived a wild cat. The cat, somehow, overheard the discussion that took place between the sparrow and the rabbit.

The cat immediately thought of a plan, took a holy dip in the river, and then sat like a priest and began chanting god's name in a loud tone. When the rabbit and the sparrow heard the cat chanting god's name, they approached him with a hope to get impartial justice and requested him to pass a judgement in the matter.

The cat became very happy to have both of them in front of him. He pretended to listen to their arguments. But as soon as the right opportunity came, the cat pounced upon both of them and killed and ate them together with great relish.

Moral—*Tussle over triffle matters may sometimes lead to a certain disaster.*

❏ ❏

65. THE CAMEL WITH A BELL ROUND HIS NECK

THERE lived a cart-maker whose name was Ujjwalaka. He was not doing well in his business. Day by day, he was becoming poorer. Seeing no way out, the cart-maker decided to settle in some other town and try his luck there.

While the cart-maker and his family were travelling through a jungle, they saw a female camel suffering from labour pains. Seeing the female camel whining in pain, the cart-maker's wife pleaded with him to detain their journey for some time so that the poor animal could be rendered some help at this vital hour. The cart-maker's family stopped there and his wife began nursing the female camel. Soon, she gave birth to a baby camel. The cart-maker and his wife took great care of her and brought her to his house along with her baby. Gradually the baby camel grew to full size.

Fondly, the cart-maker tied a bell round the neck of the young camel. Now whenever, the young camel would move around, the bell would jingle.

The cart-maker would sell the milk of the female camel and earn a lot of money. Soon he purchased one more female camel. The fortune smiled on the cart-maker and soon he became the owner of a number of camels.

All the camels used to go together to graze in a nearby jungle.

The young camel was in a habit of trailing behind other camels. This was of great concern to other camels. They advised the young camel not to stray behind. But the young camel didn't pay heed to their advice.

One day, the camels were grazing in a nearby jungle. A lion heard the jingling of the bells. He followed the sound and saw a caravan of young camels grazing. He noticed one camel with a bell round his neck, strayed behind and still eating grass. The other camels assuaged their

118

hunger and went back home. The young camel began to loiter around. The lion in the meantime, hid himself behind a bush. When the camel with the jingling bells came grazing near the bush the lion pounced upon him; killed and ate him.

Moral—*Take heed of a good advice.*

❑ ❑

66. THE LIONESS AND THE YOUNG JACKAL

LONG, long ago, there lived a lion couple in a dense forest. One day, the lioness gave birth to two cubs. Now the lion would go out hunting and bring home a prey, to be fed upon by the lioness and the cubs.

However, one day, the lion wandered for a long time in search of food, but all in vain. Soon the sun set and the desperate lion decided to return home. While on his way back home, he came across a baby jackal. The lion taking pity on the baby jackal didn't kill it. Instead, he fetched it home safely and presented it to his wife.

"My dear", asked his wife, "What's it? Is it for my meals?"

"It's a baby jackal, which I found on my way back home. I didn't kill it, because it's simply a baby. However, it is upto you; if you wish, you can kill this baby and eat it."

"Since you didn't kill this baby yourself. I too spare its life. I shall look after this baby jackal as my own third son," said the lioness. Thus, the couple decided to rear the newcomer as their own baby. She began to feed the baby jackal also on her own milk. Soon the baby jackal became fat and healthy. The three babies grew up together without realising any difference between them. The baby jackal played with the lion's cubs, as if it were one of them.

One day, while the three were playing outside their cave, they saw an elephant trumpeting near the cave. Despite the enormous size of the elephant the lion cubs became furious to see it and took an attacking posture instinctively. Whereas, the young jackal shouted, "Hold it! don't go near this huge animal. He is our enemy." Howling like this the young jackal ran back towards his home. For the first time, the cubs were face-to-face with cowardliness. This was not in their traits; but since they were young and quite inexperienced, they were discouraged to see the baby jackal running away from the battle-field. The cubs also returned home gloomy and dejected. They went to their mother and narrated to her the story of their brother's cowardice.

The young jackal was irritated to see his brothers making complaints to their mother about him. He abused his brothers in great anger and shoved them about.

The lioness sank in deep thought and decided to reveal the truth of the origin of the baby jackal to him before it was too late and became dangerous for his life. She also felt that since it was time of the growth of the cubs, and development of their natural instincts and traits, the company of the cowardly baby jackal will only hamper the prospects of their growth. So, she said to him with deep concern, "Listen son, the truth is that you are the son of a jackal. Since you were an orphan, I took pity on you and reared you as my own child. You're no doubt, smart and intelligent, but no elephants are ever killed in the family you were born in. Better you return to your clan before our sons come to know this truth about you and kill you."

The young jackal was terrified to know this truth. He immediately fled from the cave, into the deep jungle to live with his own clan.

Moral—*One should always be in ones own company.*

❏ ❏

67. KING CHANDRA AND THE MONKEY CHIEF

ONCE upon a time there lived a king by the name of Chandra. He had a beautiful palace surrounded by a huge garden. In this garden there lived many birds. Even monkeys had their homes in it. The king had also a goat for his sons to play with. The goat had long wool like hair on his body. Being a glutton he would enter into the royal kitchen and eat whatever food was stocked there. The chief cook didn't like this goat and would, sometimes, beat him with smouldering sticks to drive him out of the kitchen.

The chief of the monkeys had witnessed the scene many times. He was very intelligent. Seeing the hairy goat being thrashed with smouldering sticks almost everyday, he thought to himself: "This hairy goat, despite being thrashed with smouldering sticks by the chief cook repeatedly, doesn't shun his habit. This may become very irritating for the cooks. One day the cooks might set the hairy goat on fire. The goat might rush into the stable with his wool like hair blazing and roll onto the hay in pain and panic. As a result the hay will catch fire. Thus many horses will get burnt. And it is said that the fat of a freshly killed monkey is applied to cure the burns of a horse. If such a situation ever arises, we monkeys are sure to be slaughtered."

The chief of the monkeys, then, advised his followers to abandon the palace garden, as early as possible. But the other monkeys didn't pay heed to his sincere advice. So the monkey chief decided to himself leave the palace garden and go to some other distant place, where he would be safe and secure. So he left for a distant jungle to live in there.

One day, shortly after the goat had entered the royal kitchen, a cook picked up a burning log and struck the goat with it. The goat's hair caught fire. The goat rushed into the stable with his hair blazing. He rolled over the heap of hay to extinguish the fire but instead, the hay caught fire. The flames leapt up to the roof of the stable. Many horses were burnt to death whereas a number of them received burn injuries. The king was shocked to learn that his horses had sustained burn injuries. He called the veterinary doctor for treatment of the animals. The doctor advised the king to bring monkey fat. He said, "Your Majesty, if the fat of a freshly killed monkey is applied to the burns of the horses, they would be cured."

The king immediately ordered for the killing of the monkeys. Soon thousands of monkeys were killed and their fat was applied to the burns of the horses.

When the monkey-chief who was living in some other jungle came to know of this killing, he became very sad. He vowed to take revenge on the king.

Once the chief of monkeys went to a nearby lake to quench his thirst. There, his attention was diverted to some footprints which were all pointing towards the lake, but not a single one was pointing away from the lake. Just then, a big black giant (Rakshasa) came out of the lake's water, with a necklace of jewels round his neck. The chief of monkeys was frightened, but the black giant said, "I'm very happy with you. You were clever not to enter the lake. Whoever enters this lake is eaten by me. I can eat thousands of people at a time. I'm pleased with you. You may ask me for granting a boon to you. Please speak."

"So listen!" said the monkey chief, "I've great enmity with king Chandra. He ordered the slaughter of my brothers, for the purpose of using their fat to rub on the burnt skin of the horses."

"Bring the king and his men into this lake and I'll devour all of them," the black monster said to the monkey-chief.

"Please give me your jewel necklace," the monkey-chief said. "I'll bring you a lot of royal people for your meal."

The black giant happily gave the necklace to the monkey-chief.

The monkey-chief put the necklace round his neck and went to the king's palace. The chief of monkey told the king that there was a lake nearby and it was full of jewels. He said that he had brought one such necklace to show as sample. The king listened intently about the lake of jewels and asked the monkey-chief to tell more about it.

The monkey-chief said, "To get a jewel necklace, like the one I've, one has to take a bath in the lake before sunrise. So, please take all your men with you to the lake, Your Majesty."

The king became very happy with this invitation. The next morning he set out for the lake with his family members and hundreds of his courtiers.

After arriving at the lake the monkey-chief said to the king, "Your Majesty, wait here. Let others go into the lake first to take the necklace. Since you're a king, you'll be presented with a special necklace."

While the king waited near the lake, his family members and courtiers all jumped into the lake to collect the jewelled necklace.

The king waited for a long time for his family members to emerge out of the lake. But none of them came out.

In the meantime, the monkey-chief climbed up a nearby tree. He said to the king, "You foolish king! Your family members and courtiers, all have been devoured by the black Rakshasa living in the lake. You killed my family and I've had my revenge on you. There is a saying; 'It's no sin to return evil for evil.' I saved you because once you were my master."

When the king heard this he became sad and returned to his kingdom crestfallen.

Moral—*Tit for tat.*

68. THE ROTATING WHEEL

ONCE upon a time, there lived four friends in a village. They were very poor. They wanted to earn a lot of money, but didn't know how to do it?

After a lot of thinking they decided to leave their village and go somewhere else in search of wealth. So, after a few days of journey, they reached a place called Awanti. The four friends first bathed in the nearby river Shipra and then worshipped in a temple. There in front of the temple they met a sage named Bhairwanand. They bowed before him in respect. The sage asked, "From where have you come? What's the purpose of your visit to this town?"

"We four are friends," said one of them. "All of us are very poor. So, in a bid to try our luck we left our village, and now, we are here. Since, you are an eminent sage, we expect you kindly to help us become wealthy."

Bhairwanand was very pleased with those four friends. He gave them four cotton wicks, one to each of them and said, "Go in the direction of the Himalayas carrying the wicks in your hands. At whatever places your wicks drop, dig up that spot, collect the buried treasure whatever it is and return home."

The four friends became very happy. They set off in the direction of the Himalayas. They had hardly covered some distance in the Himalayas that the wick fell from the hands of one of the friends. He quickly dug up the spot and uncovered a treasure of copper. He invited his other companions to collect their share and return home. But his three friends called him 'stupid' and proceeded deeper into the Himalayas to find more wealth. The one who had found copper returned home cheerfully, with his wealth.

After a journey of few days, the wick of the second friend dropped on the ground. He immediately dug up the place and found a treasure of silver. He called his two friends and asked them to pick up their share of silver and return home. But the other two called him 'Stupid' and continued with their journey. The one who had dug up the treasure returned home with the wealth of silver.

After a journey of few days, the third friend also dropped his wick. He dug up the spot where the wick had fallen and uncovered a big treasure of gold. He yelled in delight and said to his last friend, "Come, let's share this booty. It's enough for two of us. Why go alone any farther."

But the fourth friend continued with his journey, saying that he hoped to find diamonds. So, the one who had found gold, returned home with the heap of gold.

The fourth friend started walking in the direction alone, where he hoped to find diamonds. But the wick he was holding, didn't fall from his hands. The fourth friend lost his way. He began wandering and was totally disorientated.

While still wandering, he came across a strange man standing at a place. His body was drenched in blood. The most strange thing was a big wheel, whirling over his head.

The fourth friend went to him quietly and asked in surprise, "Who're you and what kind of wheel is this, whirling over your head?"

Hardly had the fourth friend finished his question that the big wheel shifted its position and came straight over the head of the fourth friend, still whirling.

The fourth friend cried in pain and disbelief: "Friend, what is this? It's giving me tremendous pain."

"This wheel was attached to my head also in a similar fashion," the other man replied.

"And when will I get rid of it?" asked the fourth friend and started weeping.

"Only when someone carrying the magic wick comes wandering at this place and speaks to you," said the man.

"Please tell me how long have you been here?" The fourth friend asked still sobbing.

"Even I myself don't have the right answer to your question", replied the man. "But I came here during the reign of king Rama. I was a poor man like you. Somehow, I got a magic wick and came to this place in search of diamonds. I saw a man standing here with this wheel whirling over his head. As soon as, I put up this question, as you put up to me a moment ago, the wheel came upon me."

"How did you manage your food during such a long period?" asked the fourth friend in a trembling voice.

"You don't ever need food or water. You are also free from sleep, old age or death. You only suffer pain, for centuries, unless someone approaches you with the same magic wick. In fact, this wheel was made by Kuber to guard his wealth against the thieves and robbers. So good-bye my friend."

The man went away leaving the fourth friend with the wheel whirling over his head.

Now, when the third friend found that his friend was taking too long to return, he set out to find him. He finally arrived at the same place, where his fourth friend was standing drenched in blood, with a wheel whirling over his head.

"What is this?" he asked his fourth friend in great astonishment.

"This is the result of my greed for wealth," replied the fourth friend and narrated the whole story, weeping and moaning.

"I'm sorry to see your ill-fate, friend. But you didn't listen to me, when I offered you gold. You wanted more. Now I can only wish you all the best," said the third friend and went away with a sad heart.

Moral—*One bird in the hand is better than two birds in the bush.*

❑ ❑

69. THE PRINCE AND THE SEEDLING

ONCE there was a king whose son was very ill-tempered and bad mannered. The king, the courtiers and many other eminent citizens tried to reform the prince and make him understand the bad impression his ill manners and wicked ways would create on the public. But the prince paid no heed to their sensible advices.

One day, the king saw a sage walking in front of the palace. He had an alms bowl in his hand. The king saw his glowing face with rediance and was very much impressed with the way the sage was walking. His gait suggested that the sage was full of confidence and divine knowledge. The king asked one of his ministers to invite the sage to his court.

The sage came to the king's court. He was received with great honour by the king and his courtiers.

When the king came to know that the sage was trying to find out a good dwelling place for himself, he offered him a hermitage in his palace. The sage accepted the offer of the king and started living in the hermitage.

One day, the king said to the sage, "You would have probably come to know by now, that my son is very ill-tempered and bad mannered. The people of my kingdom call him an unworthy prince. They don't want him to succeed me as king. I request you kindly to teach the prince to mend his ways." Then the king discussed other matters of his kingdom with the sage and left his son under his direct care and guidance with a confidence that the sage will definitely ameliorate the prince and bring a positive reform in him.

The next day, the sage took the prince for a walk through the garden of the palace. Pointing to a tiny plant the sage said to the prince, "Eat a leaf of this plant and tell me how it tastes."

The moment the prince tasted the leaf he immediately spat it on the ground. "It seems to be a poisonous seedling. If it is allowed to grow into a big tree, it may prove dangerous for the health of many people." The prince pulled the tiny plant out of the ground and tore it to pieces.

Then the sage picked up the torned and mutilated plant and said to the prince, "As you've reacted in the case of this plant, the people of your kingdom may, one day, react in the same manner with you, because they think you are a wicked prince. They may not allow you to rule the kingdom and may send you to exile. So it is much better that you mend your ways to create a feeling of mercy, compassion and kind heartedness all around."

The prince understood the message of the sage. From that day onwards, he tried to grow humble and kind hearted, full of mercy and love.

The king was pleased and extremely happy to see such a big change in his son. He thanked the sage and expressed his gratefulness for his kindness.

Moral—*Bad temperament doesn't win the hearts of people.*

❑ ❑

70. THE BAD LADY AND THE WOLF

LONG ago, there lived a carpenter in a village. He was gentle but his wife was of a wicked nature and bad character. She detested her husband, because he was much older than her.

Her infidelity drove her to become friendly with some other young men. One day, she met such a man who showed interest in her. But the man was in fact a thief. He knew that she was a lewd woman and had a lot of money with her. So, with a pretension of love, he decided to rob her. He said to her, "I love you very much. I know, you too love me. Why don't you marry me. Come to me with some money. Then, we'll run away to some other town; marry there and live comfortably, thereafter."

The carpenter's wife readily agreed to his proposal. She was herself looking for such an opportunity. She decided to take away with her all the wealth of her husband.

One night, when her husband was fast asleep, she put all the gold and silver ornaments and the money in a bag and left the house. She met her thief boyfriend and they both started moving to some other town. They walked for hours and came across a river. They had to cross the river to reach another town.

As the young man had the only motive of robbing the woman of her ornaments and money, he said to her, "Darling, we have to cross this river to reach another town. We should do it immediately before the break of dawn, otherwise, we might be caught by your husband and relatives."

"But I don't know how to swim," the lady said.

"Don't worry, first I'll cross the river and deposit the wealth on the other bank of this river, and then I'll come back and carry you."

The woman gladly handed over the money-bag to the thief. The thief again said, "Take off your costly clothes also. I'll carry them safe and dry across the river."

The woman, then, took off her clothes also and gave them to the thief.

The thief took the wealth and the clothes and then walked off.

The woman, all naked, sat on the bank of the river waiting for hours and hours for the thief to return, but the thief didn't show up again.

Just then, a wolf wandered there with a piece of meat in his mouth. When he saw a fish in the river water, he put down the piece of meat and ran to catch the fish. Just then, an owl swooped down upon the piece of meat and flew away with it. On the other hand, the fish too swam back deep into the river. The wolf now had nothing to eat. The woman said to the wolf, "What'll you eat now? you've lost the meat and fish both."

The clever wolf understood all that had happened. He said to the woman, "Your condition is more pitiable than mine. I, nonetheless, would somehow, manage to get food, but what about you? You've become naked and also lost your husband, lover, the wealth and even the costly clothes. Who'll give shelter to you? Who'll accept you, now?"

The wolf went away, laughing sarcastically at the woman, leaving her to her own destiny.

Moral—*Bad deeds bring bad consequences.*

❏ ❏

71. THE USEFUL THIEF

In a town, there lived a trader. He was a middle aged man. He was rich but a widower. He wanted to marry, but no girl was willing to marry him.

After many months of bride hunting, he got married to a young girl and on this account he had to bribe her poor father with a lot of money. But the young girl didn't like the middle aged trader. She didn't allow her husband to come near her or to take her in his arms. The trader was very unhappy with this kind of attitude of his wife.

One night, while the trader was sleeping in his bed all alone, his wife came rushing to him and held him tightly in her arms. She was trembling with fear. The trader was highly surprised. Just as he took his wife in his arms he saw a thief standing in the doorway.

The trader understood everything. He said to the thief, "Friend, this young wife of mine never came near me. But today, she has taken me in her arms because of you. I am so happy with you that I am ready to give you anything you desire. You may carry anything that you wish to take with you."

"Sir", replied the thief, "There is nothing valuable in this house that I can take with me. But, in future if your wife doesn't come near you or does not hold you in her arms, I'll surely come here."

The thief then went away without taking any article from the trader's house. But from that day onwards the trader's wife treated her husband very lovingly.

72. DHARAMBUDDHI AND PAAPBUDDHI

IN a village, there lived two friends. Their names were Dharambuddhi and Paapbuddhi. Paapbuddhi was not satisfied with the wealth he possessed. Contrary to this, Dharambuddhi was not only intelligent, but had also a lot of wealth with him. Paapbuddhi made a plan to earn wealth with the help of Dharambuddhi.

One day, he said to Dharambuddhi, "Friend, why are you wasting your talent here? If you go to some other town, you may come across many opportunities to earn a lot of money and fame. If you like, I can also accompany you to the new town."

Dharambuddhi agreed to the proposal of Paapbuddhi. Both of them set out on a long journey to settle in a new town.

There, Dharambuddhi became very famous and rich in the new town.

After Dharambuddhi and Paapbuddhi had earned a lot of money, they decided to return to their home town.

As they arrived near their home town, Paapbuddhi said to Dharambuddhi, "I suppose it will be better if we don't carry all our wealth with us. Our relatives may ask for their share. Let's take a nominal amount with us and bury the rest in a pit here. When the need arises, we may come here again and take out the money from the pit.

So, they dug up a pit and after burying their wealth in it, they went to their respective homes.

But, thereafter, in one dark night Paapbuddhi visited the pit all alone and along with his money he stole Dharambuddhi's money also.

After a few days Paapbuddhi went to Dharambuddhi and said, "Friend, I need some money. Let us go to the pit to take out some money." Dharambhddhi agreed to it and Paapbuddhi and Dharambuddhi went to the spot where the wealth was buried. They dug up the pit, but there was no wealth, in the pit.

"I never did it," said Dharambuddhi in great anger. Both of them began to fight with each other and at last, the matter was taken to the court.

Paapbuddhi narrated the whole story and said to the judge, "My lord! Dharambuddhi denies that he dug up the wealth in my absence. So, in my opinion the court should hear the tree also who was the sole witness to all that happened to the wealth there."

The court agreed to this and fixed a date when the court will visit the tree to know the tree's version.

In the meantime, Paapbuddhi told his father, "Father, you know, I've stolen the wealth of Dharambuddhi. I want you to help me, or else I'll be caught and punished by the court."

"What am I supposed to do?" asked Paapbuddhi's father, "I don't want to lose the wealth."

"Well," said Paapbuddhi, "there is a Shami tree in the jungle. We had buried the wealth near this tree. The tree is hollow from inside. You just hide in the hollow. When the judges ask you to name the thief you shout from inside the tree. 'It's Dharambuddhi.' His father agreed to do it.

On the appointed day, the judge accompanied by Paapbuddhi and Dharambuddhi and other people went to the tree. Paapbuddhi then went near the tree and asked in a loud voice, "O, divine tree, tell us the name of the thief?"

Immediately, there came a voice from inside the tree, "Dharambuddhi is the thief. He has stolen the wealth."

The judge was wonderstruck to hear the tree speak.

But, meanwhile, Dharambuddhi put a heap of dry leaves and grass around the tree and lighted it. Everyone failed to understand what Dharambuddhi was upto. Soon there was a big fire around the tree trunk. After sometime, Paapbuddhi's father jumped out of the hollow of

the tree yelling for help. Half of his body was burnt and his eyes were popping out.

Now everything was crystal clear. The judge understood the whole story. He held Paapbuddhi responsible for the theft. He ordered his men of the court to hang Paapbuddhi to death by the same Shami tree.

The people were happy that Dharambuddhi, after all, got justice.

Paapbuddhi was rightly punished for his greed and dishonesty.

❏ ❏

73. THE THIEF AND THE SANYASI

ONCE upon a time, there lived a Sanyasi in a Matha. His name was Dev Sharma. He was a learned man. Many people used to visit him for his valuable preachings and advices on important matters. They presented valuables and money to Dev Sharma. After sometime, Dev Sharma became very rich. The wealth he had amassed, became a great source of worry for him. He had to guard his wealth with great care. He always kept the money-bag under his armpit and never parted with it.

Once a thief whose name was Ashadhbhuti, came to know of Sanyasi's wealth. He made a plan to steal it. And in order to materialise his plan Ashadhbhuti approached Dev Sharma and expressed his desire to become his disciple.

"Om Namaha Shivaya", said Ashadhbhuti. "Gurudev, I'm tired of this worldly pleasure. Please accept me as one of your disciples and teach me the way to attain 'Moksha'."

"My child", said the Sanyasi, "I'm pleased with your words." The Sanyasi then performed some rituals to make Ashadhbhuti his disciple.

Now Ashadhbhuti messaged his Guru's hands and feet and waited upon him to wangle his affection and favour. But the Sanyasi didn't seem to fully trust Ashadhbhuti, because he never allowed him to enter the Matha at night. He also never parted with his money-bag. This was disappointing for Ashadhbhuti. But he didn't give up.

One day, the Sanyasi was invited to a nearby village to perform ceremony of sacred thread at one of his disciple's house.

The Sanyasi took the thief along with him. On the way, they came across a river. There Sanyasi folded his money-bag in his robe and said to his disciple, "Ashadhbhuti, look after this bag very carefully while I take my bath in the river."

After sometime, the Sanyasi returned having finished his holy bath. But Ashadhbhuti was not to be found there. Only his robe was lying on the ground. He quickly checked for the money-bag, but there was no money-bag in the robe. He began to cry, "I've been robbed". He swooned and fell on to the ground.

When he regained his conciousness, he became very sad and returned to his Matha—an unhappy and dejected man.

Moral—*Wealth may sometimes prove a source of all troubles.*

❏ ❏

74. DANTILA THE TRADER AND GORAMBHA THE SWEEPER

IN a city called Vardhamana, there lived a rich trader by the name of

Dantila. He was a prosperous merchant. He kept both the common man and the king very happy. He was respected and loved by all. Even the king respected him and had allowed him free access to the palace.

Dantila had a beautiful daughter. In course of time, her marriage took place. On this occasion, Dantila invited the entire public and the king and his courtiers.

A sweeper in the king's palace by the name of Gorambha, also attended the marriage—but uninvited. He sat beside the royal family members on a seat which was meant for somebody else. Dantila caught him by his neck and beat him with a stick and told him to leave the place.

The sweeper felt insulted and decided to take revenge on Dantila.

Several days later, one early morning, when the king was not yet wide awake and Gorambha was on duty to sweep the place near the king's bed, he pretented to be drowsy and said, "This Dantila is a very cunning fellow. He poses as a gentleman, but, in fact, has an affair with the queen."

When the king heard these words, he got up immediately from his bed and asked Gorambha, "Gorambha, is that true?"

"Master," said Gorambha, "when I am very much tired, I just mutter in my drowsiness. I don't know what I've been saying."

But the king was not satisfied with his answer. He thought, Gorambha was hiding some facts. From that day onwards the king withdrew his favours from Dantila. He was forbidden to enter the palace. Dantila was perplexed. He couldn't make out as to why the king's behaviour had changed suddenly.

One day, Dantila and Gorambha came face to face outside the palace. Gorambha laughed sarcastically when he saw Dantila. Dantila quickly realised the reason behind the cold behaviour of the king.

The next day, Dantila invited Gorambha to his house. He gave him a pair of garments and coconut and said, "My dear friend, I'm sorry for my behaviour that day. But you must realise that it was entirely wrong on your part to take a seat, which was reserved for a Brahmin. The Brahmin felt insulted, and that is the reason why I'd to throw you out. Please forgive me."

Gorambha was happy to receive the gifts. He said to Dantila. "Sir, Let us forget the past. This is my assurance that you will once again enjoy the favours of the king."

The next day, he went to the palace and started sweeping the floor. After sometime, he again pretended to feel drowsy and when he became sure that the king was lying half awake, he muttered, "The king is very dirty. He eats cucumber in the toilet."

When the king heard this, he got up and sat straight on his bed and said to Gorambha, "What did you say, you stupid? When did you see me eating cucumbers in the toilet?"

Gorambha pretended as if he was frightened. "Your Majesty," he said in a quivering tone , "when I'm overworked, I feel drowsy during the day time. I start muttering in my sleep. I've already told you about this. I really don't know what I was muttering."

When the king heard this, he was left in a profound thought: "This Gorambha is an idiot. He mutters lies in his sleep. As I've never eaten cucumber in the toilet, so in the same way it is quite possible that Dantila too had never had an affair with my queen."

After having considered this carefully, the king invited Dantila to the palace. He presented him with jewels and clothing and Dantila's former status was regained.

Moral—*No one is high or low. So we must never insult anyone.*

❑ ❑

75. THE COW AND THE TIGER

Long, long ago, there lived four cows in a jungle. They were fast friends. They always grazed together and saved each other when some wild animal attacked them. This was the reason why even tigers, and lions couldn't gather the courage to kill them and eat them.

A lion had, indeed, an eye upon these cows. But he could never find the right opportunity to make them his prey.

One day, the cows fell out. Each one grazed separately her own way. This was the right opportunity for the lion to attack them. So, the lion hid himself behind the bushes and when a lonely cow would come closer to the bushes, he would pounce upon her and kill her for his meals. In this way, all the four cows were killed one by one by the lion.

Moral—*Unity is strength.*

❑ ❑

76. THE FOOL AND THE CROOKS

LONG, long ago, there lived a foolish man in a village. He was such an idiot that even a school child could fool him easily. The fool had one horse and one goat, as his pets.

One day, the fool decided to sell his horse and the goat in the market. He tied a bell round the neck of the goat with the help of a thin string and tied the other end of the string to the horse's tail. He then, mounted his horse and set out for the market place.

Some crooks who knew the fool very well, made a plan to get the horse and goat for their own use. So, one of the crooks, on the way, untied the bell from the goat's neck and, instead, tied it with the horse's tail. The fool didn't ever realise what went on behind his back. The bell tied to the tail of the horse went on ringing and the fool believed that all was well.

On the way, another crook asked the fool to stop and look behind. When the fool looked behind the crook said, "Sir, how is it that you have hung a bell by your horse's tail? What purpose does it serve?"

The fool was already shocked to find the goat missing. He became very sad and proceeded to the market place.

In the meantime, the third crook came near the fool and said, "Sir, I've seen a man running away with your goat. If you like, I'll chase the thief on your horse and get back your goat?"

The fool became very happy to hear this. He immediately got down from his horse and handed it over to the third crook. The crook now mounted the horse and drove away.

The fool waited and waited for his goat and the horse to come back, but it never happened.

The crooks, thus, stole the fool's horse and the goat leaving the fool in the middle of the road crying for help.

Moral—*A fool and his wealth don't stay together for a long time.*

❑ ❑

77. COURTESY

Once upon a time, there lived a poor Brahmin in a village. He used to perform poojas and hawans in the nearby villages. Once another Brahmin came to his house and said, "I've to perform some pooja. Will you kindly allow me to stay in your house for a few days?"

The Brahmin gladly received him and allowed him to stay in his house.

One day, the Brahmin said to his wife, "Today is Sankranti. See that our Brahmin guest is fed well. A guest is equivalent to God. So be courteous to him."

The Brahmin's wife became angry to hear this and said, "It's not enough to be courteous only. There must be something in the house to offer to the guest for eating. Unfortunately, I've nothing in my kitchen to offer. Besides, you never made ornaments for me nor did you ever buy good clothes for me. Such is the situation in this house. And you ask me to take full care of your guest."

She argued with the Brahmin but he kept his cool.

The Brahmin consoled his wife, "Dear, I know, we're poor but even then we should offer some food to our guest. It's more of the expression of our good feelings than the real food."

Then the Brahmin's wife said, "I've a little sesame seed in the house. I'll make some dish of it and offer to the Brahmin guest."

She prepared the sweet dish from the sesame seeds and offered it to the guest.

Moral—*Courtesy is the sign of good behaviour.*

❑ ❑

78. THE MERCHANT'S SON

LONG, long ago, there lived a merchant by the name of Sagaradatta. He had a son. The son once bought a book of poems. He recited a line of the poem so many times that he came to be known as, 'You get what you are destined to.'

One day, a beautiful princess by the name of Chandrawati went to a festival in the city. There the princess saw a handsome prince and fell in love with him. Not being able to check her emotions, she said to her maid servant, "Find some way for me to meet this prince."

The maid met the prince and gave him the message of the princess. The prince agreed to meet the princess. He asked, "But where and how do I meet the princess?"

"Well," said the maid, "when it's dark you come to the white palace. There, you'll find a rope hanging from one of its windows. Climb up this rope to reach the princess' room."

But on the appointed day, the prince backed out. He didn't turn up.

Meanwhile, 'you get what you are destined to' came wandering near the white palace. He saw a rope hanging there from one of its windows. He climbed up the rope and entered the room of the princess. As it was dark, the princess could not see the face of 'you get what you are destined to.' She thought that it was the same prince with whom she had fallen in love. She entertained him lavishly and talked to him for a long time, but the so called prince kept mum for all the while.

"Why don't you speak?" asked the princess.

"You always get what you are destined to," answered the merchant's son.

Hearing this the princess took a closer look at the merchant's son and soon realised that she was all through talking to a wrong man. She became furious and turned him out of her chamber.

Then 'you get what you are destined to', went to a nearby temple and slept there.

The watchman of the temple had an appointment with a woman of bad character in the same temple. So he requested the merchant's son to go and sleep in his quarter, which was situated in the rear side of the temple.

'You get what you are destined to,' instead, entered a wrong room. There the watchman's daughter Vinayavati was waiting for her lover. As it was pitch dark, she could not recognize the merchant's son and married him in the room itself according to Gandharva rites. Then she said, "Why don't you talk to me?"

"You get what you are destined to," replied the merchant's son.

Vinayawati soon realised that she had been talking to a wrong man. So, she kicked out the merchant's son out of her house.

When he came out, he joined a passing marriage procession. The name of the bridegroom was Varakeerti.

When the marriage ceremony was about to start, a mad elephant, who'd already killed its master, appeared on the scene. Every one ran helter-skelter to safety.

Then 'you get what you are destined to' rushed to the brides help. He drove the elephant out by jabbing a long nail into its head. When the bridegroom returned and saw 'you get what you are destined to' holding his 'would-be' bride's hands he became angry. But the girl said that since 'you get what you are destined to' had saved her life from the mad elephant, she would marry him only.

And this girl was the same princess who had mistaken 'you get what you are destined to' for the prince, who she had been waiting for in her room in the palace and after coming to know the truth, had kicked him out.

The whole city came to know about the girl's decision.

The king also came to know of his daughter's love.

Then, the king with great pomp and show married the princess with 'you get what you are destined to' and both of them lived happily, thereafter.

So, at last, he really got what he was destined to.

Moral—*Destiny plays an important role in life.*

❑ ❑

79. THE POTTER'S TRUTH

Long, long ago, in a village there lived a potter by the name of Yudhisthira. He was in a habit of drinking liquor. One day, he stumbled on a broken pot in a drunken state and fell down. The sharp edge of the broken pot pierced his forehead and he started bleeding profusely. He didn't care much for his wound. The wound got worse. Even after it had healed, it had left a big scar on his forehead.

After sometime, there was a famine in the country. The potter lost his business. He, then, left for some other part of the country. There he, somehow, got himself employed in the king's service.

Once, the king noticed the big scar on the forehead of the potter, he thought to himself that the potter must be a brave man. The scar was most probably the result of his face to face fight with some soldier of the enemy.

So, the king decided to place the potter amongst his chosen army generals. As the war was impending, the king decided to bestow honour on generals to encourage them.

Later the king decided to make the potter the chief of the army. So he asked the potter, "General, what's your name? How did you get this scar on your forehead? What was the name of the battle you fought in?"

"Your Majesty," replied the potter, "I'm a potter by profession. Once I fell down on a broken pot in a drunken state and got wounded. This scar is the result of that wound."

101 Stories from Panchatantra—9

Hearing this, the king was very much dejected. He ordered his soldiers to throw the potter out of the army.

The potter begged for king's forgiveness. He requested the king to keep him in royal service, so that he could prove his worth in the army, but the king refused and sternly ordered his expulsion from the army and the kingdom.

Moral—*If you speak the truth, sometimes it may go against you.*

❏ ❏

80. KING NANDA AND VARARUCHI

ONCE upon a time, there lived a king, by the name of Nanda. He was very brave. His fame spread far and wide. Many kings of the neighbouring kingdom bowed before him.

The king had a minister called Vararuchi. He was an expert in politics and a scholar of Sanskrit.

Once Vararuchi's wife became very angry with her husband. As Vararuchi loved his wife very much, he said to her, "Darling, what is it that makes you so angry? I'm ready do anything to make you happy."

"Then get your head shaved and fall at my feet, if you really wish to make me happy," said his wife flippantly.

Vararuchi did exactly as desired by his wife. His wife became happy and normalcy was restored in their life.

One day, king Nanda's wife also became angry with her husband. She refused to talk to the king. King Nanda also loved his wife very much. "Darling!" he said to his queen, "Tell me what is it that I can do to make you happy?"

"Well," replied the queen, "I'll put reins on your mouth, ride you like a horse. You must also neigh."

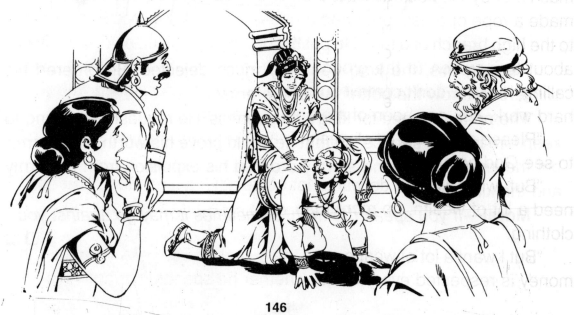

The king did exactly as desired by the queen. The queen also became happy and things became normal.

The next day, the king was sitting in his court. His minister Vararuchi came to him. The king looked at Vararuchi and laughed at him, "Vararuchi! why've you shaved your head all of a sudden? What's the reason?"

Vararuchi replied, "Your Majesty, I've shaved off my head for the same reason for which you neighed like a horse yesterday."

The king simply simpered. He could not utter a word.

❏ ❏

81. SOMILAKA THE WEAVER

LONG, long ago, there lived a weaver in a town by the name of Somilaka. The cloth he wove was so fine and beautiful that even the king liked it. But, somehow, he still remained a poor man, while other weavers were quite rich, even though they wove inferior cloth. This bitter fact made Somilaka sad. He left his native village and went to settle down in some other town to try his luck . In this town also, Somilaka couldn't earn much money. He became frustrated and decided to commit suicide. He made a rope of grass, prepared a noose and tied the rope's other end to the high branch of a tree. He put the noose round his neck. As he was about to jump on to the ground, he heard a voice from the heaven calling, "Hold it, don't commit suicide. It is I, God. I'm pleased with your hard work. Ask any boon of me and I'll grant it."

"Please give me a lot of wealth," said Somilaka. He was astonished to see God before him.

"But, what will you do with a lot of wealth?" asked God. "You don't need a lot of wealth, no more than what is required for your food and clothing."

"But I want a lot of wealth even then," replied Somilaka. "A man with money is respected everywhere, whether he spends it or not."

147

Seeing that Somilaka was adamant on his demand, God said, "First go to your native town and meet the two traders living there. One is known as 'Secret Wealth' and the other as 'Useful Wealth'."

Somilaka became very happy. He went back to his native town. There he decided to first observe the 'Secret wealth's living.

When 'Secret Wealth' saw Somilaka, he became very angry. He talked to Somilaka in an abusive language. 'Secret Wealth's wife offered him food in a broken plate. She also banged the glass of water on the floor. Somilaka didn't utter a word. He ate his food and thanked the family members of 'Secret Wealth' and left quietly. Then he went to meet 'Useful Wealth' trader.

'Useful Wealth' was much delighted to see Somilaka. Even the other members of his house welcomed him. They served him with delicious food. They talked to him in a friendly tone. At night, proper arrangements were made for him to take rest.

Early next morning, the king's servants arrived and brought money for 'Useful Wealth.'

When Somilaka observed this, he thought to himself: "This 'Useful Wealth' is not a wealthy man, but even then he lives more comfortably than the 'Secret Wealth'."

His wish for a lot of money was granted by God. He began to enjoy his wealth to the full, just like 'Useful Wealth.'

Moral—*Wealth must be used properly. Where necessary it must also be donated.*

❑ ❑

82. THE DOG IN A FOREIGN COUNTRY

LONG, long ago, in a town, there lived a dog by the name of Chitranga. Once there was a famine in the country. Due to lack of food the animals began to starve and die. Chitranga too began to starve. So he went to a foreign country for food and water.

Reaching the foreign country, Chitranga began to wander in search of food. At one place because of the negligence of the lady house holder the door of a house was left without being locked properly. Chitranga got into the house and fed himself on various kinds of delicious food. This became his daily routine. But, after he would come out of the house, the other dogs on the street would chase him and bite him all over his body.

Chitranga became very sad. He thought to himself: "It's better that I return to my own country and live in peace, in spite of the famine."

So, Chitranga decided to return to his own country. When Chitranga arrived in his country, his friends and relatives surrounded him with curiosity and asked him many questions relating to his foreign travel.

Then Chitranga said, "In foreign countries the housewives are in a habit of leaving the doors of their houses open. One can enter the house freely and eat a lot of food in the kitchen. But there is one disadvantage; your own relatives and friends bite you to death."

❏ ❏

83. THE DEVTA AND THE WEAVER

ONCE upon a time, there lived a weaver by the name of Mantharaka. One day, while he was weaving, his handloom broke down. So he decided to go to a nearby forest to cut wood and bring it home to repair his handloom. The weaver, then took an axe and set out to the forest.

While he was walking on the seashore looking for a good tree, he came across a Shinvashapa tree. He decided to cut it down to repair his loom.

As soon as, the weaver started cutting down the tree with his axe, he heard a voice saying, "Stop! please don't cut this tree. It's my home."

"So What!" the weaver said. "I've to repair my loom, otherwise, how will I weave the cloth and sell it in the market to feed my wife and children. Please find some other tree to live in."

As soon as, the weaver raised his axe to strike again at the root of the tree, the voice requested yet again, "Please spare this tree. I am very pleased with your answer. Ask for a boon and I'll grant it."

"That's fine, but let me consult my wife and friends and then I'll let you know about my wish."

"Well," said the tree devta, "do it and come back to me."

The weaver returned to his town. There he consulted his friend, a barber. After listening to the whole story the barber said, "It would be wise of you to ask for a kingdom. Once the boon is granted you will become a king and there will be no scarcity of any kind in your life. And then I hope you will make me your prime minister."

"This is all right, but let me consult my wife also. She loves me very much."

"Don't do this. The shastras advise against consulting women, because of their lower level of intelligence."

But the weaver went to his wife. He narrated the whole story to her. "Tell me," the weaver asked his wife, "what boon should I ask for? My friend, the barber has advised me to ask for a kingdom."

"Your barber friend is a fool," said his wife.

"Kingdoms have always been a source of trouble. You'd have to fight battles to defend your kingdom. You'd have to look after the welfare of your people. Rama had to go into exile. Ravana was destroyed. It's for the sake of kingdom that brothers, sons and other close relatives plot to kill each other. So, its better that you ask for something, which'll bring more benefits to us. You may ask for two more hands and one more head, so that you could weave more cloth and earn more money by selling more cloth in the market."

The weaver then approached the tree devta and told him about his wish. The devta fulfilled his wish. The weaver got two extra hands and one extra head.

But while the weaver was returning home full of joy, the town people saw him and got frightened. They thought him to be some kind of a monster. They began pelting stones at the weaver and killed him.

When the barber came to know about the death of the weaver, he became very sad.

Moral—*An advice should never be followed blindly.*

❑ ❑

84. THE FOUR FOOLISH BRAHMINS

ONCE upon a time, there lived four Brahmin friends in a village. They were learned persons, but were not satisfied with the knowledge they possessed. So one day, they decided to join some good university in some other part of the country for the sake of learning.

The next day, they travelled to Kanyakubja. There they got admission in the university. They studied at the university for ten long years.

One day, they said to each other, 'We've now acquired enough knowledge of Sanskrit and other subjects. Let us go back to our native village.'

The four learned friends, then, set off for the long journey. After travelling for hours they arrived at a place, where two roads met. The four pandits got puzzled. They didn't know which road to follow. At the same time, a funeral procession passed by on its way to crematorium. There were some prominent citizens walking along with the procession. One of the Brahmins consulted his shastras: 'Follow the road, which is followed by eminent people.' So all of them started following the procession.

When they reached the crematoruim, they saw a donkey standing there. They didn't know what to do with the donkey. So the other Brahmin took out his Shastra and began to read it: 'Whosoever meets you at the crematorium is your true friend.'

And so, while one of the Brahmins put his arms round the donkey's neck, the others touched his feet with respect. Just then, they saw, at a distance, a camel moving quickly towards the crematorium. The third Brahmin, then consulted his books, which said: 'Religion spreads rapidly. It must be tied with something friendly.'

So the four Brahmins thought, that the camel was the religion because it was walking swiftly and so the friendly donkey should be introduced to the camel—the religion. When the camel came nearer, they tied its neck together with the donkey's neck.

When the owner of the donkey, a washerman, came to know of this, he picked up a stick and started chasing the Brahmins. All the four Brahmins ran for their lives.

While being chased by the washerman, the four Brahmins came to a river. There in the river, they saw a Palash Leaf floating on the surface of water. One of the Brahmins said, "This leaf is like a raft. It'll save our lives." And with these words, he jumped on to the leaf. As a result, the Brahmin began to drown as he did not know how to swim. The second

Brahmin, then, caught hold of his hair and said, "When a thing is going to be fully destroyed, a wise man saves at least half of it." So he cut the drowning Brahmin into two halves with a sword.

The remaining three Brahmins proceeded further on their journey. They reached a village, where they were welcomed by the villagers and invited for lunch and dinner.

One of the Brahmins was served with a noodle like long substance. The Brahmin, then, consulted his Shastras and read out the verse, which said : 'Anything lengthy is a cause of destruction.' So he didn't take his meal and went away hungry.

The second Brahmin was served a coconut dish in his lunch. Seeing the dish, the Brahmin remembered the verse that said : 'Frothy things have temporary life.' So, the Brahmin left his food and went away without eating anything.

The third Brahmin was served with a dish round in shape. Seeing the hole in the middle of the cake like round rice and pulse dish, the Brahmin thought of the verse which meant : 'the holes are like defects and are a sure sign of approaching disaster'.

So, the third Brahmin also left the village without taking his meals.

In the end, the three learned idiots had to go hungry for days till they returned to their native village.

Moral—*Theoretical knowledge without the practical experience and commonsense is useless.*

❏ ❏

85. TWO FISH AND A FROG

LONG, long ago, there lived two fish and a frog in a pond. The names of the two fish were Shatabuddhi and Sahasrabuddhi. The name of the frog was Ekabuddhi.

One day, when the three friends were talking to each other on the edge of the pond, some fishermen passed by. They were carrying baskets and nets with them. They saw the pond and said to one another, "This pond seems to be full of fish. Let's come tomorrow and catch them."

When the fishermen left the place, the frog said to the fish, "Friends, you also heard what the fishermen said. Let's leave this pond immediately and go to some other pond to save our lives."

But the two fish laughed. Sahasrabuddhi said, "Well, as far as I think the fishermen will never come back to catch us. But even if they do, they'll never be able to trap us, because we're expert swimmers and we know how to save ourselves."

But the frog was not convinced with the views of the fish. He said, "But I find myself not so expert in swimming. I'll definitely leave this pond along with my family by this evening, to settle down in some other pond or well."

The same evening, the frog abandoned the pond along with his family and went to a nearby pond. The next day, the fishermen came to the pond. They cast their nets and caught all the fishes. The two fish tried to escape, but in vain. They also got trapped in the net and died.

When the frog and his wife saw the fishermen returning with a lot of fish in their net, they became very sad. They looked at the net with tearful eyes as they saw that their two friends, Shatabuddhi and Sahasrabuddhi also had succumbed to death.

Moral—*One should not turn a deaf ear to a friend's advice.*

❏ ❏

86. THE MERCHANT AND THE BARBER

ONCE upon a time, there lived a merchant called by the name of Manibhadra, in a town known as Patliputra. He was of a charitable nature. But, somehow, due to misfortune, he lost all his wealth and became a pauper. His status in the society gradually came down. He became sad and dejected.

One night, as he lay in his bed, he started cursing his fate and thought of committing suicide by starving himself to death.

While thinking thus, he fell asleep. A jain monk appeared in his dream and said to him, "Don't worry! I'm wealth, gathered by your forefathers. You are their legitimate heir. It's your legal right to possess me. Tomorrow, I shall come to your house in the guise of a jain monk. Just hit me on my head with a stick and I'll turn into solid gold."

The next morning, when the merchant woke up he felt pain in his head. He didn't believe his dream. In the meantime, his wife had called in a barber to massage her feet. Soon after the arrival of the barber, a jain monk came to the merchant's house. The merchant welcomed the monk. He offered him seat and a glass of water. Then he hit the monk's head with a stick. The monk fell down and turned into gold from head to toe.

The merchant picked up the gold and hid it in a basement room.

The barber who was a witness to all this thought to himself: 'I'll also invite these magical monks to my home to dine with me. When they come, I'll hit them on their heads, to turn them in gold. Soon I'll be a wealthy man'.

Then the barber went to the head monk and invited him and other monks to his house to dine with him. But the head monk refused the invitation. He said, "We are no Brahmins, who're invited to the houses to eat. Everyday, we collect alms and accept food only from the first devotee of the day. We eat to live only and not live to eat."

The barber then waited outside the monastery. When the monks came out, he requested them to come to his house and conduct prayers. A few monks agreed to it and went to the barber's house.

As soon as the monks entered the house, the barber hit them on their heads with a heavy stick. A few monks died, whereas a few others were badly injured.

The news of the barber hitting the monks spread in the town like wild fire. The barber was arrested by the authorities and taken to the court of law.

The judges, in the court, asked the barber, "Why did you do this?"

The barber then narrated the whole story. He said, "I did it because I saw the merchant doing it."

Then the merchant was ordered to appear before the court. The merchant narrated the whole story.

The judges then ordered, "Let this wicked barber be hanged till death." The barber was then hanged to death.

Moral—*A blind imitation is always dangerous.*

❏ ❏

87. THE BATS

Long ago, a fierce fighting broke out between the beasts and the birds. The birds pecked at the beasts and flew away. The beasts were helpless as the birds used to fly out of their reach after pecking at them. This battle went on for many days. The bats on their part kept themselves aloof. They didn't join either the birds or the beasts. They preferred to go with the winner. They thought to themselves: "Ours is a special position, we're birds because we can fly, we're beasts because we don't lay eggs". The bats only watched the birds and the beasts fight with each other.

So the fighting went on. Seeing the birds in a winning position, the bats would join the birds, and the next time they would support the beasts, because the beasts seemed to be winning.

On the other hand, the birds and the beasts seemed to have become tired of their continuous battle. So, they decided to make peace. The king of birds and the king of beasts both sat together to find out some way to a permanent peace. Ultimately, both of them decided to forget the past and become good friends. They also decided not to allow the bats community either to join the birds or the beasts, because they were opportunists.

At last, the bats were left alone. They felt ashamed of themselves. They hid themselves in the dark caves and crevices. They came out of their hiding only at twilight—when the birds were back to their nests and the beasts were not yet out of their dens.

Moral—*One should avoid fair-weather friends.*

❑❑

88. THE LION'S BAD BREATH

LONG ago, there lived a lion in a dense forest. One morning his wife told him that his breath was bad and unpleasant. The lion became very angry and got embarassed to hear this comment. He wanted to check this fact with his councillors, as well. So he summoned them one by one to his court.

First came the sheep.

"Hello friend sheep," said the lion, opening his mouth wide, "tell me, if my mouth smells bad?"

The sheep thought that king lion wanted an honest answer from him, so he said, "Yes, Your Majesty. There seems to be something wrong with your breath."

This plain speak did not go well with king lion. He pounced upon the sheep, killed him and ate him.

Then king lion called the wolf and said, "What do you think? Have I a bad breath?"

The wolf knew the fate his colleague, the sheep, had met. He wanted to be very cautious in answering a royal question.

So, the wolf said, "Who says that Your Majesty's breath is unpleasant. It's as sweet as the smell of roses."

When the king lion heard the reply he roared in anger and immediately attacked the wolf and killed it. "The flatterer!" growled king lion.

Finally, came the turn of the fox, who was lion's third councillor.

When the fox came, the lion asked him the same question.

The fox was well aware of the fate of his two colleagues. So he coughed and cleared his throat again and again and then said, "Your Majesty, for the last few days, I have been having a very bad cold. Due to this, I can't smell anything, pleasant or unpleasant."

The king lion spared the fox's life.

Moral—*One should keep quiet in the times of danger.*

❏ ❏

89. THE WIND AND THE SUN

ONCE an argument took place between the wind and the sun as to who was stronger of the two. The wind claimed that he was stronger than the sun, whereas, the sun disagreed saying that he was more powerful than the wind.

Of course, this was a friendly argument, but there seemed to be no end to it. After a marathon discussion, they both came to the conclusion that mere discussion won't serve any purpose. They, practically, have to do something to prove their point.

Just then, they saw a traveller walking down the road. The sun got a bright idea and said to the wind, "Let's test our strength on that man. Whosoever of us can force him take off his jacket, shall be considered the winner. Have your chance first."

Saying this the sun hid himself behind clouds and got ready to see the fun.

The wind took the first turn. He blew an icy blast. But the harder he blew, the more closely did the traveller wrap his jacket around his body. The wind tried everything; clung to every ruse. He heaved his stormy power from all sides, but all in vain. His confidence in his mightiness began shattering gradually. And ultimately, out of sheer disgust and embarassment the wind gave up.

Now it was the sun's turn. He gently put aside the patch of cloud which served as a veil a moment ago. The anthelion around the cloud disappeared and now the sun was in the open field with all his vigour. He began to shine with all his might. The traveller felt the warmth of the sun. Then gradually the sun grew hotter and hotter. The traveller first loosened his jacket and then finally, took it off. He began to perspire. He sat in the shade of a tree and fanned himself.

Thus, the sun proved himself to be stronger than the wind.

Moral—*Persuasion can achieve, what a brute force can't.*

❏ ❏

90. THE RICH MOHAN AND THE POOR SOHAN

LONG ago, there lived two friends in a village. They were known as Mohan and Sohan. Mohan was a jeweller and was very rich, while Sohan was very poor. Once on the occasion of his sister's marriage, Sohan took a few gold ornaments worth rupees five thousand from Mohan and promised to pay the price of it within six months from the date of buying on credit.

But only a few days after the marriage of Sohan's sister, Mohan began asking for the money which he was supposed to get from Sohan for the gold ornaments bought by him on credit.

"You know, I am a poor man," said Sohan. "How can I make the payment so soon. Moreover, if I remember correctly, I had already told you that I shall be able to pay you back in six months' time. Anyway please give me some more time. I'll pay the money."

But Mohan had an evil design on Sohan's properties. He wanted Sohan to sign some documents in the court of law, saying that he mortgaged his house and other properties against the gold ornaments.

Sohan again pleaded his helplessness, but Mohan was adamant on his demand.

So, seeing no way out Sohan said to Mohan, "How will I go to the court? I don't even have a horse to reach the court."

"You can take my horse to ride to the court," said Mohan.

"I don't have nice clothes to wear," said Sohan.

"You can put on my clothes," said Mohan.

"I don't even have shoes to wear," said Sohan.

"Take my shoes," said Mohan.

Now Sohan agreed to go to the court. He put on Mohan's clothes and shoes and rode to the court on Mohan's horse.

When the judge called the name of Sohan, he said, "My Lord, I want to ask Mohan certain questions."

"Go ahead," said the judge and ordered Mohan to answer to the questions put up by Sohan.

"Tell me, Mohan," asked Sohan, "to whom do these clothes, I'm wearing, belong?"

"They're mine," replied Mohan.

"To whom do these shoes, I'm wearing, belong?"

"They're mine," said Mohan.

"And the horse that I rode to the court?"

"The horse too belongs to me," shouted Mohan.

The people present in the court began to laugh.

Sohan said to the judge, "My Lord, you can yourself judge the mental state of Mohan. He thinks everything that I possess belongs to him only."

The judge also laughed and dismissed the case saying that Mohan had lost his mental balance and has started thinking that everything that Sohan owned belonged to him. Thus, Sohan foiled Mohan's evil designs.

Moral—*Greed is evil. It must be destroyed with shrewdness.*

❏ ❏

91. THE WOLF AND THE LAMB

LONG ago, there lived a wolf in a dense forest. The forest was surrounded by hills and gorges. A small river flowed through it.

Once the wolf was drinking water at the head of a stream, when he saw a lamb drinking water from the same source down at some distance. The cunning wolf began to think of an excuse for attacking the gentle lamb and eating him. So he shouted down at the lamb, "How dare you make the water dirty I am drinking?"

"You must be mistaken, sir," said the poor lamb gently. "How can I be making your water dirty, since it flows from you to me and not from me to you?"

The wolf began thinking cunningly of some other ruse in order to make an issue and get a justifiable excuse to kill the lamb and eat his delicious flesh.

"Do you remember having applied all sorts of contemptuous and even abusive epithets to me, just a year ago?" said the wolf to the innocent lamb.

"But, sir," replied the lamb in a trembling voice, "I wasn't even born a year ago."

"Shut up, you fool," shouted the wolf again. "Do you think I'm a fool? If it was not you then it must have been your father, who abused me long ago."

"At the most, I can apologise on behalf of my erring father if he at all ever did so," pleaded the lamb trembling.

"I think you're the kind of fellow who first commits a sin and then tries to argue it out. Let me teach you and your family a good lesson", saying this the wolf jumped upon the poor lamb and tore it to pieces and ate it.

Moral—*Any excuse will serve a wicked person.*

❏ ❏

92. THE GIANT AND THE HELPLESS BRAHMIN

ONCE a Brahmin was passing through a jungle to reach another town, when a huge and cruel giant hiding somewhere behind the thick bushes, attacked the Brahmin and jumped upon his shoulders. The giant dangled both his legs in front of the Brahmin and sat comfortably on his shoulders.

The Brahmin began trembling with fear, but he was helpless. He didn't know what to do. The giant said to the Brahmin, "I'm very fond of human flesh. But before killing and eating you I wish to have a joy ride on your shoulders. So take me where I say."

The Brahmin had no choice, but to obey the giant. So he kept on walking. While walking the Brahmin noticed that the giant's feet were extraordinarily small and soft. The Brahmin asked the giant, "I'm very surprised to see that you're so huge, but your feet are so small and delicate. How is it?"

The giant thought, there was no harm in revealing the secret of his feet to Brahmin since very soon the Brahmin is going to be killed and eaten up by him. So he said, "I never walk on ground with my feet wet. Walking or running on wet feet gives me great pain."

The Brahmin kept the giants words firmly in his mind and kept on walking. After walking quite a distance they reached on the banks of a river. The giant said to the Brahmin, "Let me down here and you yourself stay here, till I come back, after taking my bath."

The Brahmin became very happy seeing the giant taking a dive in the river. By the time the giant took another dive in the water, the Brahmin took to his heels and ran away to save his life.

The giant saw the Brahmin running away from the river bank, but he could do nothing to stop him. He was wet all over because he was taking his bath. In this situation, with his feet wet the giant was quite helpless to chase the Brahmin. Thus, the Brahmin escaped from the clutches of the giant and saved his life.

Moral—*It always pays to be alert.*

❏ ❏

93. THE BRAHMIN AND THE DIAMONDS

ONCE upon a time there lived a clever Brahmin in a village. He performed poojas during the day time and robbed the unsuspecting travellers during the night time. Thus, by adopting unfair means and indulging in criminal activities, he had collected a lot of wealth.

One day, a few merchants from some other town came to the village. They sold all their belongings and purchased six large size diamonds. On their return journey again they had to cross the jungle. So to save the diamonds from bandits they swallowed them up.

The Brahmin had already seen the merchants hiding the diamonds in their stomachs. He decided to steal the diamonds. He went to the merchants and became friends with them. He read out religious scriptures like the Veda before them and soon won their confidence. He now waited for the right opportunity to steal the diamonds.

As the merchants and the Brahmin were passing through the jungle, it became dark. They saw a tribal village nearby. They also heard the crows cawing. The shrewd Brahmin knew that the crows were informing the tribals about the presence of wealth with the merchants. The tribals understood the language of the crows. They came running with sticks and spears and attacked the merchants and the Brahmin. They searched the merchants clothes and luggage, but couldn't find the diamonds. But since the tribals were convinced of the presence of the wealth with the merchants, they decided to kill all of them and the Brahmin too.

Knowing their evil intention, the Brahmin thought that if they killed a merchant and found the diamond in his body, they will kill him too and

165

all the other merchants. So the Brahmin said to the tribal chief, "You kill me first. If you find the diamond in my body, kill the rest of my brothers. Otherwise let them go away. So the tribal chief killed the Brahmin. He slit his stomach, but could not find any diamond. So he allowed all the other merchants to go home.

The tribals returned to their village. They were surprised. They thought, either the crows had begun telling lies, or they failed to interpret their language correctly.

Moral—*To sacrifice ones life for others is a great deed.*

❏ ❏

94. THE GIANT AND THE HORSE THIEF

LONG ago, there lived a king by the name of Bhadrasen. He had a beautiful daughter, whose name was Ratnavati. Besides these two, there was the third, a giant, living in the nearby forest. The wicked giant had evil designs on princess Ratnavati. The giant loved her and wanted to marry her. But he was unable to lay his hands on the princess because she wore an amulet round her neck, which saved her from all the evils. The giant used to come to the room of the princess and embarrass her in many ways.

Once the giant entered the room of the princess and hid himself behind a long curtain. He heard the princess talking to her friends and saying, "I'm very much pestered by a powerful giant everyday. Can you suggest some way to kill him?"

When the giant heard the words 'powerful giant' he became worried. He thought that the 'powerful giant' must be some other very strong giant who wanted to kidnap the princess as he himself wanted to do. The giant now wanted to catch the other powerful giant and kill him. The giant, then, by his magical powers transformed himself into a horse and began to stay in the stable with other real horses.

One night, a horse thief entered the stable and began looking for the best horse to take along with him. He chose the 'giant horse' and drove away with it.

Now the giant thought that the rider was himself the 'powerful giant'. So the 'giant horse' got frightened. The thief whipped the 'giant horse' and the horse ran faster than before. After sometime, when the thief wanted to stop, he pulled the reins, but the 'giant horse' wouldn't stop. The thief tried his level best to stop the horse, but in vain. Then he came to realise that in fact the horse he was riding was actually a giant because each time he pulled the reins it increased its speed instead of slowing down.

Now trying to find a way to escape from the running 'giant horse', the thief jumped and caught hold of a thick branch, overhead, of the banyan tree when he passed under it. The horse went running straight in his speed. The thief became happy to have escaped like that.

On the banyan tree, there lived a monkey who was a friend of the giant. He knew that the giant had mistaken the rider to be a more powerful giant. So, the monkey, in order to make the giant aware of the fact, said to him, "Why do you run frightened from the human beings?"

The giant understood everything and stopped to kill the thief and eat him. Just then the thief who was hanging by the branch of the tree bit hard the tail of the monkey, which was dangling in front of his face.

The monkey shrieked in pain. The giant once again got confused and thought that the thief was really a 'powerful giant' and would surely kill him. And so, he ran away to save his life.

The thief also jumped down from the tree and went home.

❏ ❏

95. THE VILLAGE MOUSE VISITS TOWN MOUSE

ONCE upon a time, there lived a gentle mouse in a village. He had a friend living in a distant town. One day, the village mouse invited his town living friend to his village home to wine and dine with him. When the town mouse came to the home of the village mouse, the village mouse opened his heart and soul in the honour of his town friend. The village mouse served a variety of tasty dishes to his town friend.

The town mouse, although shared the delicious dishes with his village friend, but he still showed his dislike for the rural atmosphere. "How do you live here in this village, my friend. It's living like a toad in a well. Can you ever prefer this village to the excitement of the city?" You're simply wasting your time and energy here. Come to town some day. I'll show you what's life." Then the town mouse thanked his village friend for the fine invitation and returned to his home town.

After sometime, the village mouse went to see his town friend. The town mouse lived in a big house, in the heart of the city. He lived especially in a banquet hall, where dozens of delicious dishes were served to party of revellers and other guests.

The town mouse served dozens of delicious dishes to his village friend on a huge table.

While the two mice were engaged in enjoying the food, they heard a sound of barking and growling outside the banquet hall.

"What is that?" asked the country mouse.

"Oh! just nothing," said the town mouse. "These are only the master's dogs barking for nothing."

But the country mouse was not satisfied with this answer. Just then the door of the banquet hall flung open. A party of dancers, together with four huge dogs entered the room. The frightened friends jumped off the dining table and hid themselves in a far corner of the room.

When the things calmed down and the dancers went away with their huge dogs, the two friends came out of the hiding, still trembling with great fear. The country mouse bidding 'good-bye' to his friend said, "If this is the fine way of living in the city, which is full of terror, I would best prefer to have only my simple barley bread in my village where there is peace and security, to your dainty dishes with a sword always hanging above your head. You're always welcome to my village home, my friend.

The village mouse once again thanked the city mouse and came back to his sweet village home.

❏ ❏

96. THE THIEF, THE GIANT AND THE BRAHMIN

LONG ago, there lived a poor Brahmin in a village. He used to perform poojas in the nearby villages to earn his living. Once a rich farmer gave him a cow and told him to sell cow's milk in the market to earn part of his livelyhood. But the cow was very weak. The Brahmin then begged for alms and fed the cow. Soon the cow became fat and healthy.

Once a thief saw the fat cow of the Brahmin and decided to steal it. One night he headed towards the Brahmin's house.

A giant also used to live somewhere near the village. He devoured human beings. The thief met this giant, while he was on his way to Brahmin's house to steal his cow. The thief asked the name of the giant. The giant replied, "I'm Maharakshasa. I eat humans. Today I'm going to devour the Brahmin. But who're you by the way?"

"I'm a big thief. I steal whatever I like. Today, I've decided to steal the Brahmin's cow."

"Come on then!" said Maharakshasa. "Let's go together to the Brahmin's house."

So, both of them reached the Brahmin's house together. The Brahmin was deep asleep at that time. The thief whipped out a big knife from his pocket and started walking to the place, where the cow was tethered. But the giant blocked his way.

"Wait friend!" the giant said. "First let me eat this Brahmin."

"No!" said the thief. "It's quite possible that while you go to eat the Brahmin, he wakes up and runs away. In that case there might be quite a commotion here and as a result, neither you'll get your Brahmin nor will I get my cow."

169

And thus, both of them started having a heated argument between themselves. The loud arguments woke up the Brahmin. He soon

realised the whole situation. He recited mantras and burned the Maharakshasa with his spiritual powers. Then he started beating the thief with a long and thick stick. The thief began to cry and ran to save his life. Thus, the Brahman was saved from the giant, as well as, from the thief.

Moral—*Quarrelling on any issue always benefits the others.* ❑❑

97. THE BRAHMIN AND THE DELICIOUS DISHES

LONG ago, there lived a Brahmin in a village. He was a simple and honest man. But his wife was of a bad character. She had developed an illicit relation with a charming youth of the village.

When the Brahmin was away, the youth would visit his wife and make love to her. The Brahmin's wife would cook delicious dishes for her lover. Then they would talk and enjoy the food together.

Once, while she was cooking a variety of dishes, the Brahmin got suspicious and asked her, "Why are you preparing all these dishes?"

The Brahmin's wife said cleverly, "I'm going to offer these dishes to the temple of a goddess. It's situated on the outskirts of the village."

But the Brahmin was not satisfied with his wife's answer. When her wife left for the temple of goddess carrying with her all those dishes she had cooked, he too reached the temple taking some other route. He reached the temple before his wife and hid himself behind the statue of the goddess.

After sometime, his wife came to the temple and began to pray to the goddess. "O, mother goddess, please help me in getting rid of my wretched husband. He is an obstacle in my love. I wish to make him blind. Kindly bless me."

The Brahmin who was hiding behind the statue of goddess, changed his voice to mimic a lady and said, "O dear lady. I'm very pleased with your worship. You've brought so many tasty dishes to offer to me. Now listen to me carefully. Make such delicious dishes daily and serve them to your husband. One day, he'll surely go blind."

She was happy because once her husband, the Brahmin, went blind, there would be no obstacles. She would meet her boyfriend in the presence of the Brahmin and he won't know anything about it. Her boyfriend won't have to wait for the Brahmin to go out of the house before coming to make love to her. The Brahmin's wife was extremely glad to hear the goddess speak thus to her. From that day onwards she prepared delicious dishes daily for her husband to eat.

After months of eating delicious food, the Brahmin, one day, started to stumble on everything that he came across. He pretended to have gone blind and said to his wife, "Look dear, what's happend to me? I can't see anything. Perhaps I've lost my eyesight."

Listening to this, his wife began to dance in delight. She informed her lover too of this incident. He quickly reached at her beloved's house to make love to her. As soon as the youth took the Brahmin's wife in his arms, the Brahmin came there and opened his eyes. Then he beat the youth with a stick till he died. He chopped off the nose and ears of his wife and kicked her out of the house.

Moral—*God doesn't help in sinful acts.*

❏ ❏

98. BRAHMADATTA, THE CRAB AND THE SNAKE

ONCE upon a time, there lived in a village, a youth by the name of Brahmadatta. One day, Brahmadatta had to go to some other town for some important business. His mother called Brahmadatta and said to him, "My dear son, don't travel alone. Better take a companion with you. He can help you, at least, when you are in trouble."

But Brahmadatta said, "Mother, I am a young man. I can very well take care of myself. Besides, who do I take with me as companion?"

"I'll manage a companion for you," said Brahmadatta's mother. She, somehow, fetched a crab and put it into Brahmadatta's travelling bag. As Brahmadatta didn't want to hurt his mother's sentiments, he kept the crab into a camphor box and started on his long journey.

Brahmadatta, walked for days to reach the other town. He became tired and wanted to take a little rest before starting his journey again.

So, Brahmadatta lay under a huge banyan tree and soon went to sleep.

In the hollow of that banyan tree, there lived a snake. Seeing Brahmadatta fast asleep, the snake climbed down the tree and went near Brahmadatta's travelling bag. The snake was attracted to the box of camphor, which was kept in the bag.

As soon as the snake entered the camphor box, the crab sitting inside caught hold of the snake's neck and killed it.

When Brahmadatta woke up, he was surprised to find a dead snake lying beside him. Now he remembered his mother's advice—Take a companion with you. Don't travel alone.'

Moral—*It is advisable to have a companion while moving to an unknown destination.*

❏ ❏

99. THE PRINCE AND THE BEAR

Once a prince went to a jungle to hunt for animals. He wandered the whole day in search of prey but to his sheer disappointment and disgust he didn't get a single animal, big or small. He became tired and sat under a tree to take rest. Just then he saw a tiger coming towards him. The prince got frightened and scrambled up a tree. There he saw a bear already sitting on a branch. The prince got badly terrified because, up there in the tree was sitting a bear and down on the ground was the tiger. The prince began to tremble with fear. But the bear said to the prince, "Don't worry, my dear prince, I'll not harm you, you're my guest." The prince believed in what the bear said. But, the tiger was still waiting for him on the ground.

Soon the sun set and since, the prince was terribly tired of whole day's wandering, he fell asleep. The bear gave him support with his body to enable him to lie down comfortably on the branch. Then the tiger said to the bear, "This is a human being. Human beings are our enemies. Throw him on to the ground for my meals."

"I'll not throw the prince on to the ground, howsoever bad he might be," said the bear. "Moreover, he is my guest."

In the morning, when the prince woke up, he saw the bear sleeping beside him. The tiger said to the prince, "Don't trust this wicked bear. He's showing all his sympathies to you because I am sitting here. He'll not spare you, once I leave this place. It's my humble advice that you push this bear down before me. I'll eat him and let you go."

The prince believed in what the tiger said and pushed the bear off the branch. But the bear was alert. He caught hold of another branch of the tree and saved his life. He cursed the prince for his unthoughtful act and said, "We animals are better than you human beings."

Moral—*Animals too are lovable and understanding.*

❏ ❏

100. THE CROW AND THE WATER PITCHER

LONG ago, there lived a crow in a jungle. Once he was wandering in search of water to quench his thirst. At last, he came flying over a village. There he saw a pitcher lying in front of a house. There was some water in it. The crow tried to reach the water, but couldn't succeed. The water level was too low in the pitcher. The crow began to think of some practicable device and finally came up with a bright idea. He looked around and found a pebble. He picked up the pebble in his beak and dropped it into the pitcher.

The crow realised that the water level had risen a little. So he dropped more pebbles in the pitcher till the water level was high enough for his beak to touch it.

The thirsty crow then drank the water to his hearts content and flew away.

Moral—*Necessity is the mother of invention.*

❏ ❏

101. THE HORSE AND THE LION

LONG ago, there was a farmer who had an old horse with him. As the horse had become old, the farmer told the horse to leave his house and live in some forest. The horse became very sad. He said to his master, "Master, I'm your old servant. I have served you all my life. I have always been faithful to you and there has been no slackness on my part in carrying out my duties. So long as I was physically strong, you had all your affections for me but as soon as you realised that I have become physically infirm; I, no longer, have that vigour and vitality in me, you asked me to leave your house and go and live in some forest. Is this a reward to the services rendered by me with all my honesty and faithfulness?"

The farmer was at a loss of words. He had no logical answer.

"All right!" the farmer said to the horse. "You can stay in my house provided you bring me a lion. I want a lion's skin."

So the worried horse set out for the forest. There he met a fox. The fox took pity on the horse and enquired from him the reason of his sadness. The horse narrated the whole story.

The fox being good natured offered to help the horse. He said to the horse. "You lie down here on the ground as if you were dead."

The horse followed the advice of the fox and lay there on the ground as if he were dead.

Then the fox met king lion and said "Your Majesty, there is a dead horse lying in an open field. It's better you come and see for yourself."

When the fox and the lion reached the spot, where the horse was lying pretending to be dead, the fox said, "Let us pull this horse and put it behind the bushes so that we could have a peaceful meal. What I'll do is that I'll tie your tail to the tail of the horse."

"Yes, I agree with you," said the lion.

So the fox, instead of tying lion's tail to that of the horse, tied the horse's tail with the leg of the lion. Then he asked the horse to get up and run fast.

The horse, at once got up and started running as fast as he could.

All this happened so suddenly that the lion didn't get a chance to balance himself. The horse was running so fast that he was literally being dragged like a dead animal. His body slammed against big rocks so many times and was caught by thorny bushes in the way. He was getting injuries after injuries and was bleeding profusely.

The lion began to cry and threaten, but the horse didn't stop. At last, the lion couldn't take any more of it and succumbed to injuries.

The horse stopped at his master's house with the dead lion tied to its tail. The farmer was very happy to see the dead lion. He permitted the horse to stay at his house as long as he wished.

Moral—*Mind is mightier than body.*

❑ ❑ ❑